THE CHOCOLATE CHALLENGE

A NOVEL BY
DAPHNE BENEDIS-GRAB

SCHOLASTIC INC.

FOR KHAI

CHAPTER 1
MONDAY, DAY 1

"Welcome, everyone, to the kickoff of the tenth-annual Scottsdale Town Chocolate Challenge!" shouted Ms. Chase. The students gathered in the Granville Elementary School auditorium cheered, stomping their feet and high-fiving their friends.

All the students but Evan Black.

"Is everybody ready for the biggest and best chocolate sale in the history of our town?" Ms. Chase asked.

Scottsdale's two elementary schools, Granville and Deerfield, had a friendly rivalry. And that rivalry heated up every year in November when the Chocolate Challenge began. At Deerfield, where Evan had been a student for the past six years, the Challenge was the most eagerly anticipated event of the year. It appeared it would be the same here at Granville, though of course Evan wasn't sure. As the new kid in sixth grade—the *only* new kid—it was hard to be sure of anything.

"Now, I know all of you love every kind of Fantastic Five bar," Ms. Chase said, her voice going melty, which was understandable because the five kinds of chocolate bars, available only during the Challenge, were scrumptious. "But I think the S'more bar is the very best. Who's with me on that?" She held her microphone out toward the auditorium.

The room erupted as everyone began cheering for their favorite of the Five. Evan joined in with the students chanting, "Sweet and Simple, Sweet and Simple!" That was the rich milk chocolate bar that Evan had been looking forward to devouring for weeks. Next to him a group of girls shouted in support of Lava bars, a thick milk chocolate shell encasing a buttery caramel center that was also utterly delicious. Behind him a group yelled in support of the Toffee Crunch, while the entire row in front of him clapped for the Triple Crown. It was complete chocolate mayhem, and Ms. Chase grinned as it reached a fever pitch, then raised her hands to indicate it was time to settle down.

"We have exactly four and a half weeks to sell as many

of the Fantastic Five as we can," Ms. Chase went on. "And after the Challenge is complete, the winning school will get a big pizza party on the final day before winter break."

The thing was, the winning team was always Deerfield. That was totally fine with Evan back when he was a student there, but now it was not so great. Yet another reason why transferring from Deerfield to Granville at the start of the year had been hard.

Of course, Evan had known it would be. At Deerfield, Evan had made his name as a jokester. He and his friend Ian had gotten their start back in third grade, when their attempt to stick a pencil through a bag full of water during a science experiment resulted in an impromptu sprinkler that cracked up the entire class, including their teacher. That kicked off Evan's successful pranking career. He pulled off stunts like leaving fake melted ice cream puddles in gym lockers and lending pens that spurted grape juice in the middle of class. Evan was the prank king of Deerfield Elementary School, a title he wore with pride . . . until the ghastly day this past summer when a prank went so wrong Evan could barely think about it without hyperventilating. After that unspeakable incident, Evan hung up his pranking crown for good.

Now at Granville, Evan had promised himself he'd be prank-free. But he also hadn't made any friends. His parents thought he hadn't made friends yet because he hadn't joined any Granville clubs—they didn't have debate, his activity back at Deerfield, and he wasn't really into sports or theater. But Evan suspected the real reason he didn't have friends yet was that he'd given up pranks. Without them, he simply didn't stand out at a school where everyone had known each other since kindergarten.

Evan scooted to the edge of the hard wooden seat. Today things would change. It was time to be interesting again— and the key to that was the Challenge.

Ms. Chase continued. "In addition, I'm happy to announce that this year, if we win, the money from both schools' sales will go to the Scottsdale Community Center. The center acts as a vital part of our town life by offering classes to all ages, as well as hosting the annual Scottsdale musical and all our town meetings."

Evan applauded along with everyone else. The celebration where the winning team presented the check to their chosen charity happened in the town hall and was almost as exciting as the pizza party.

"Before the sale begins, we have to choose co-captains who will run the Challenge! Their responsibilities include keeping track of our sales numbers and developing our sales strategy," Ms. Chase said.

Evan sat up straight, his stomach a tangle of knots. He was excited *and* nervous. This was the moment he'd been waiting for. *This* was how Evan was going to make friends. He'd been pretty good at selling bars last year, so he'd decided that being Evan "Sales King" Black would finally get him noticed at his new school. Okay, it didn't sound quite as good as Evan "Prank King" Black, but obviously he needed to be *something* if he wanted to finally have some friends.

"As you know, we usually take a vote. But this year only two people signed up, so we won't be having an election," Ms. Chase said.

Evan nearly toppled out of his seat at this announcement. The news was both shocking and a wonderful stroke of luck. Shocking because back at Deerfield at least fifteen sixth graders ran for the honor of being co-captains, and wonderful because this meant—

"I'm pleased to introduce your co-captains, Phoebe Washington and Evan Black! Come on up here!"

Evan's heart was racing as he got to his feet and walked on slightly shaky legs down the aisle to the stage. Phoebe walked ahead of him, her head held high. Evan recognized her from his math class. She was tall with short black curls, and always had the right answer in class. Once, she had even corrected their teacher when he accidentally called the greatest common factor the least common multiple, two concepts that still confused Evan.

"These are the folks who will be handing out sales sheets every day and organizing where fifth and sixth graders will sell boxes of Fantastic Five around town." Ms. Chase gestured at Phoebe and Evan. "I'm sure with the two of them at the helm Granville will have their best Challenge ever! Please give them a hand."

Evan looked out at the students who filled the auditorium, his heart rate settling back down as he drank in the applause. It was probably the first time half of them had even noticed he was a student here. Evan turned to grin at Phoebe. She nodded but didn't grin back. Her mouth was pressed together and her eyes were serious. Evan hoped he hadn't done anything to upset her.

"Your sales team will set up their headquarters in room one-twelve." Ms. Chase flashed them a smile. "So everyone needs to stop by this afternoon to find out our sale strategy and get those sales sheets."

Evan had learned that Granville was organized like Deerfield, with two co-captains in charge of sales sheets and keeping a list of local businesses that the fifth and sixth graders, the only grades allowed to sell chocolate around town, would visit.

"Go, Team Granville!" Ms. Chase finished, pumping a fist.

With that, the kickoff event was over and students began making their way out of the auditorium.

"I know you will do Granville proud," Ms. Chase said, coming over and patting both Phoebe and Evan on the back. "And just remember, the important thing is that no matter which school sells the most boxes, we *all* win because a charity in our town gets more funding and everyone gets to enjoy the Fantastic Five."

Evan nodded. Ms. Chase was right—that *was* what mattered.

But then he noticed the corners of Phoebe's mouth turning down. A tiny flicker of worry brushed at the back of Evan's neck.

When the bell rang for lunch, Evan hurried to the cafeteria. He was greeted by the steamy scent of the day's hot meal: fish sticks and Tater Tots. Evan skipped *that* line and grabbed a turkey sandwich instead, then paid for it at the register. This was usually the moment when he had to decide whether it was more humiliating to sneak his lunch into the library or sit alone at a cafeteria table, pretending he didn't care that no one sat with him. But today he was spared that fate—today he was a co-captain of the Granville sales team and that meant he was needed in room 112, their headquarters, to begin plotting their sales strategy with Phoebe.

"Hey, aren't you one of the co-captains for the Chocolate Challenge?" a boy asked as Evan walked down the hall.

Evan grinned—already being a co-captain was getting him noticed! Friends were sure to follow, especially once he dazzled everyone with his sales skills.

"Yeah," Evan said.

"You're new, aren't you?" the boy continued. "Did you move here from China?"

Evan tried not to sigh at this question. For some reason people often assumed that because he was Asian, he was from China, when in fact, his family had lived in America for generations, and his grandparents were from Kazakhstan and Korea, not China.

"No," he said, then shifted back to the matter at hand. "I think Granville's going to win the Challenge this year."

"Cool," the boy said, raising his hand to high-five Evan.

Evan was grinning again—yes, he was on the way to making friends for sure.

Phoebe was already there when he arrived in the small classroom. It held a big table with two old computers, a whiteboard, several desks set in a circle in the center of the room, and along the back wall, a stack of Fantastic Five boxes. *Yum!* Maybe after he ate his sandwich he could sample one of the bars.

"Hi," Evan said.

Phoebe was taping a sign to a plastic bin and barely looked up. "Hi," she said, her voice muffled because she had a second marker between her teeth.

"How can I help?" Evan asked, ready to get down to business.

Phoebe removed the marker and adjusted her sparkly blue headband. "This will be for the sales sheets for the younger kids," she said, gesturing at the box that was now clearly labeled "Grades K–4." The younger grades only sold to friends and neighbors, while fifth and sixth graders were allowed to sell bars in town.

"Can you make the sign for the upper grades?" she asked, passing Evan the marker that had not been in her mouth, thank goodness, and a sheet of paper.

"Sure," Evan said. The first step toward becoming sales king was getting along with his co-captain.

"I'll label the box where people can turn in their sheets once they're all filled out," Phoebe added. "And we can put all three of them on the table so they're easy to get to."

"Sounds good," Evan said, appreciating how organized she was. He made his sign, then glanced at the sales sheets, which were identical to the ones Deerfield used: spaces for the name of the business, the names of each person ordering at the business, how many boxes they wanted of each flavor, and the total amount of money they owed. Boxes had ten bars each, and at two dollars a bar, the sale of one box was an even twenty bucks. People paid when they came by the school to pick up their boxes the day after a purchase (or the same day if there was a special request), and back at Deerfield that part had been handled by the main office. Volunteers delivered boxes to the office based on sales sheets so that pickup ran smoothly. Evan figured it would be the same here so that there was no chance of money getting misplaced or lost in the chaos of their classroom headquarters.

Phoebe had finished labeling her box and was now unfolding the town map. She spread it out on the table, then smoothed it flat.

"Should we start figuring out our sales?" Evan asked, coming to stand next to her so he could look at the map of Scottsdale. The town was a grid, with Blossom Boulevard marking the exact center. The small downtown occupied just a few blocks around Blossom. Each business was marked with a blue square on the map.

Phoebe didn't respond, and Evan saw that she was once again frowning.

"Is something wrong?" he asked, hoping the answer would be no.

But Phoebe kicked at the table leg as she stared at the map. "Granville has never won the Challenge."

"Yeah, that's tough," Evan said awkwardly, not sure if now was the time to mention that he had enjoyed Deerfield's winning ways for six years. "But maybe we'll get lucky this year."

Phoebe looked up at him, her brown eyes serious. "It's not about being *lucky*," she said. "There's no way Granville can win, not the way the contest is set up."

"What do you mean?" Evan asked. He had never heard anyone say anything like that before.

"It's right here," Phoebe said, pointing to the map. "Each school is allowed to sell on one side of Blossom Boulevard. Since our school's on the west side of town, we sell on the west side."

"Right," Evan said, trying to be agreeable even though he had no idea where she was going with this.

"But the biggest businesses, the ones that buy the most boxes of chocolate, are on the east side," Phoebe explained.

Evan looked at the map, but the number of businesses on each side seemed to be pretty even—in fact, there might have been a few more shops on the Granville side.

"I don't know," he said hesitantly.

"Then you're not looking carefully," Phoebe said impatiently, reminding Evan of how she sometimes spoke in math class when people in her work group weren't staying on task. "Deerfield has the town hall, which is easily the biggest sale of all. And they also get the hospital, which is the second biggest."

This was true—Evan and Ian had done the town hall sale last year, and it had been almost sixty boxes, an incredible tally. But still, Granville had plenty of good sale opportunities—they probably just hadn't taken advantage of them. That was something Evan could help with, to kick off his new reign as king of sales. Before he could say this, though, Phoebe went on.

"If only we had one of those two sales," she said. "That would even out the playing field and make the Challenge a fair contest for the first time in its entire history. Then we'd have an actual shot at winning."

Evan did not like the direction the conversation had taken.

"But you guys have the police and fire station—that's a really major sale," Evan pointed out. "If you take advantage of places like that, really maximize each sale, I'm sure Granville has just as good a shot to win as Deerfield."

Phoebe was looking at him very carefully. "What do you mean, 'you guys'?" she asked, raising one eyebrow.

Uh-oh. Evan's face heated up again. He could tell he was turning a rosy shade of red. "It's just—I'm new this year," he stammered.

"I know," Phoebe said. "We have math together, remember?"

"Right, yeah, but I used to go to Deerfield," he blurted out. Since they'd be working closely together it would come out sooner or later. "My family moved across town over the summer, so I had to switch schools."

Phoebe's other brow flew up. "*You* used to go to *Deerfield*," she said.

"Yeah," Evan said. "I was actually the one who sold to the town hall last year," he couldn't help adding. "It was the biggest sale in the history of the Challenge."

Phoebe nodded. "So then you see what I mean about the playing field not being even."

"No, not—" Evan began, but Phoebe held up a hand.

"How many boxes did you sell at the town hall?" she asked.

Evan suddenly felt like he was up on a witness stand being cross-examined. Phoebe was definitely intense. "Um, fifty-nine."

"And how many did the Deerfield team sell at the hospital?" she went on, now tapping her nails on the map.

"Fifty-one," Evan said. He remembered the number exactly because his nemesis, Julie, had taken that sale and claimed it was actually more impressive than the town hall sale because it had gone up 20 percent from the year before while the town hall had only gone up 11 percent. Julie was used to winning everything and could be very annoying about it.

"So that's one hundred ten boxes sold in two sales," Phoebe said, her math skills on display. "And do you know what our biggest sale was, at the police and fire station? Thirty-seven boxes," she answered before he could respond. "And do you know what our second-biggest sale was?"

She took a step toward Evan. She was now so close that he could see each bead in her sparkly headband. Evan took a step back as he shook his head. Phoebe wasn't just a little intense—she was intimidating.

"It was at the real estate office and we sold thirty-one boxes there," Phoebe said. "Our two biggest sales only got us sixty-eight boxes, forty boxes fewer than what Deerfield got for its two biggest sales. And with that kind of deficit, there's no coming back, especially since the rest of the businesses are pretty equal on both sides of town."

She was right—a gap that big could not be filled, no matter how many smaller sales Granville managed to pull off on their side of town.

"Oh. That's not fair," Evan said as it all sunk in.

"I know it's not," Phoebe agreed.

"We should tell Ms. Chase," Evan said.

"Actually," Phoebe said, "I have a better idea."

CHAPTER 2

MONDAY, DAY 1

Gabe and the rest of the students at Deerfield had cast their votes for co-captains of the Chocolate Challenge during homeroom and then waited all morning for the results to be announced. When static finally crackled over the loudspeaker, everyone in Gabe's chocolate-crazy science class quieted to hear who the winners were.

"I want to thank everyone who ran to be co-captain of the tenth-annual Chocolate Challenge," Principal Martin began.

Gabe now held his breath as he waited—but unlike the other students who had signed up to run, Gabe was hoping his name would *not* be called.

"And now," Principal Martin said, "it's my pleasure to tell you who is going to be leading us this year."

Next to him Gabe could see Willa Scott crossing her fingers.

"Julie Winthrop," Ms. Martin called out.

This was not a surprise. Julie was the star of debate, competitive dance team member, and honor roll student. Of course she won. It was the other slot that had Gabe worried.

"And she will be joined by Gabe Menendez," Ms. Martin concluded.

Gabe sighed, though it wasn't that big a shock. After all, he had led both the baseball and soccer teams to the state playoffs in the last year. Of course people wanted him as co-captain—he was a winner.

"Dude, awesome!" Gabe's friend Joe called out, as most of the other students in the class, even Willa, offered smiles and thumbs-ups.

"Thanks," Gabe said, knowing Joe was just being nice. It wasn't his fault Gabe didn't want the job.

Not that it was a bad job exactly. It was just that being the co-captain of the Deerfield sales team seemed like it would be too much work. It would take away from his time to prepare for basketball season! But after what

Gabe considered to be a very minor incident on the soccer field a few weeks ago—a slight scuffle between Gabe and another player that was truly no big deal (and the other player had been completely and totally wrong anyway)— Gabe's parents and coaches had decided that Gabe needed to participate in a less competitive, more "community building" activity.

Gabe was not really a fan of this idea. He liked winning, whether it was sports, family game night (which his parents called off over the summer after Gabe accidentally tipped over the Monopoly board when his brother, David, won— but won by cheating, Gabe was sure of it), or video games. There was nothing wrong with that, though—winning was good. And, really, was there anyone who *liked* losing? Of course not.

But Gabe's parents and coaches had made it clear that it was time for Gabe to "tone down his competitive edge," and they all agreed being a co-captain of the Challenge would help.

When class let out, instead of heading to the cafeteria with Joe, where they'd talk video games and sports with Khai and Erlan, Gabe had to drag himself to room 103, the Deerfield sales headquarters.

He wasn't surprised to find Julie already in the room setting up boxes with sales sheets. Sixteen desks were in a circle for meetings, and the teacher desk was piled with forms and a big box for turning them in. The whiteboard would be where they kept track of their sales. The main offices of each school updated the sales numbers on their websites every morning, and so Gabe and Julie would also write down Granville's numbers in order to keep an eye on the competition. There were a few school computers along the side wall in case they needed to look anything up. And stacked against the back wall, away from any sun that might shine through the windows, were big cardboard boxes filled to the brim with the Fantastic Five.

"Hey, Julie!" Gabe said. "Need help with anything?" The faster they finished, the faster he'd be back in the cafeteria talking about movies and NFL standings.

Julie turned and smiled at him. Gabe didn't really know Julie. Everyone knew *of* Julie of course—she was the person who aced every assignment, won every competition, and had been the first-ever fifth grader voted head of student council. With Julie in charge, this would probably be the best Challenge ever. And hopefully the easiest.

"I think I have the room set up and ready for this afternoon," Julie said. "I expect we'll be pretty mobbed, which is great. We want to start strong and finish strong."

That made sense.

"I don't think Granville will offer up any real competition, but of course we'll make sure we cover everything," Julie said. "I mean, obviously we'll win, but it would be great if we win by the biggest margin ever."

"Or sell the most boxes of chocolate ever," Gabe said, getting into the spirit of things. He had not thought about the Challenge as a real competition, but now that Julie had presented it that way, Gabe was excited. Winning big and setting a record—that would be awesome.

"Exactly," Julie said, smiling. "So now we just need to come up with our sales strategy."

"What do you mean?" Gabe asked. "Don't we just go to stores and ask if they want to buy any chocolate?"

"Yeah, but we want to maximize each sale," Julie said. "Sell as many boxes as possible at each one."

"I know what 'maximize' means," Gabe said, slightly irritated. He might not ace all his classes, but he wasn't an idiot.

"Sorry, I didn't mean to sound like Ms. Dunbar," Julie said. Ms. Dunbar was their English teacher, who was always modeling new vocab words. Gabe couldn't help grinning at the comparison.

"Okay, yeah, we should definitely *maximize* every sale," Gabe said. "How do we do it, though?"

"Well, we make sure to go to each and every business on our side of town," Julie said. "No matter how small."

"That makes sense," Gabe said. He thought about it a little more. "But we should go to the biggest sales first, to lock them down."

"Agree," Julie said. "The biggest sales are always the town hall and the hospital, and I think the two of us should handle them since they're so important."

Gabe nodded in approval. He liked being on the field for the game-changing plays.

"And I also had this other idea," Julie went on, going over to one of the Fantastic Five boxes. Gabe saw it was his favorite, the S'more bar, a silky shell of milk chocolate encasing a fluffy marshmallow core and studded with graham cracker chunks. Gabe was suddenly in desperate need of one, but of course he'd spent his allowance on an online upgrade of Radioactive Zombie Kill Zone, which had been totally worth it but now left him with no way to buy a S'more bar. He'd have to bring home a sheet tonight to get his parents to buy some boxes—ideally a year's supply.

"So you know how as soon as you see one of the boxes of bars, you want one?" Julie asked, taking a S'more bar out.

"Yes," Gabe said, surprised. Had she just read his mind? "Yes, I do."

"Well, what if we don't just bring the sales sheet when we're selling boxes around town?" Julie said, her eyes lighting up. "What if our sales people bring a box along so that people realize how much they need our chocolate?"

"And need a lot of it," Gabe said, grinning. "Like an entire year's supply."

"Exactly," Julie said.

"You know, maybe we could also sell single bars," Gabe said. Single bars were sold in school, and once a complete box had been sold, it was added to the tally. Given how easy it was to find two dollars for a delicious chocolate treat, the sales added up fast. But single bars had never been sold around town before, at least not that Gabe knew of. "That way people could eat some chocolate right away and then once they tasted how good it is they'd probably sign up to buy even more boxes."

"Oh, I like that," Julie said. "I know it would work on me." She looked down at the box of S'mores. "Just talking about it makes me want one now."

"Me too," Gabe said. "And the S'mores are my favorite."

"I love the Triple Crown best," Julie said, now looking at the pile of Triple Crown, a dark chocolate bar with a liquid chocolate center that was packed with moist chunks of chocolate fudge.

"That one's good too," Gabe said. All the Fantastic Five were amazing. He was about to suggest they open up a box and split a bar (maybe Julie would pay since he was broke) when the bell rang, signaling the end of lunch.

Gabe was surprised the time had gone so fast. But he'd been enjoying himself. It turned out that being co-captain was going to be a lot more fun than he'd thought.

This chocolate sale was another opportunity to win!

CHAPTER 3

MONDAY, DAY 1

"Are you sure this is a good idea?"

Phoebe sighed and pulled her turquoise-and-plum scarf a little tighter around her neck to protect it from the icy breeze blowing through downtown Scottsdale. She was getting tired of Evan asking her that question.

"Yes, I'm sure," she said as they walked down Blossom Boulevard. Phoebe had not known what to think when Evan, a quiet kid in her math class, was appointed co-captain of the Challenge with her. Evan was new to Granville this year, which made him an unknown quantity. And so far, the facts she had gathered were not adding up in his favor. Yes, Evan was nice enough and he had been helpful getting their sales headquarters ready at lunch. But

now he was making things difficult, and it was cold outside, and they had to move fast. Phoebe was starting to
worry that Evan was going to be a negative factor in her
quest to finally give their school a fair shot at winning.

"I just think it's important to follow the rules, you
know?" Evan said in a tentative voice.

"Not when the rules are unfair," she said, trying to stay
patient.

"But if we break the rules, it won't be fair either," Evan
said, almost pleading this time.

"The rule of where we can sell Fantastic Fives doesn't
take all the factors into account," Phoebe said. "So we
have to take care of it ourselves."

The door to Blackbird Bakery opened, letting out
Phoebe's neighbor Ms. Redmond, along with a warm swirl
of butter, sugar, and lemon. Phoebe wished she'd grabbed
a snack on the way out of school. But she and Evan had
been in a rush—if they were going to go through with her
plan, they had to do it before Deerfield got there first. And
with a lot more enthusiasm from Evan.

"Hi, Phoebe," Ms. Redmond said, shifting a big pink
cake box under her arm while she pulled on her gloves.
"This is for the anniversary party. I hope your family likes
carrot cake."

"Yes, ma'am, we do, and we're looking forward to the

party," Phoebe said, sensing an opportunity. A sales opportunity. "And you know what else your guests might like? Some chocolate. We're selling Fantastic Five bars to raise money for the community center."

"Oh, wonderful," Ms. Redmond said. "But I thought you went to Granville. Isn't it Deerfield that always wins?"

Phoebe did her best not to scowl, but it was hard. When even old people like Ms. Redmond, who was over forty and hadn't been in elementary school in forever, knew Deerfield always won, it was bad.

"But I'd love to buy a box from you," Ms. Redmond said, redeeming herself in Phoebe's eyes. "You can put me down for the ones with caramel."

"The Lava bar," Phoebe said, nodding approvingly. The Lava, with its satiny caramel core, was sheer perfection and Phoebe's personal favorite of the Fantastic Five.

"That was awesome," Evan said as Ms. Redmond headed down the street. "Maybe we should try to make more personal sales like that one. Then we wouldn't have to sell outside our territory."

Phoebe gritted her teeth. How many times was she going to have to explain to Evan that the only thing that wasn't right was how the contest was stacked against Granville? The contest was unfair, and nothing—*nothing*—upset Phoebe more than an unfair situation.

Phoebe's parents often told Phoebe she should be a lawyer because ever since she was young, she had argued passionately for things to be fair. On the third day of preschool, Phoebe had been outraged to discover her cup of pretzels had only seven pretzels while her friend Trina had eight, so Phoebe had appointed herself snack boss, carefully monitoring the teacher in charge of preparing snacks for the rest of the year. At home, Phoebe was always quick to point out ways that her parents favored her older sister, Audrey. Sometimes her parents responded appropriately, like making sure each sister got the same number of birthday presents each year. Other times, though, they were unreasonable, like when they forbade Phoebe from setting a timer at dinner to make sure Audrey didn't get more minutes to talk about her day than Phoebe. Her parents explained that while sometimes things weren't exactly fair in the moment, they'd often even out in the long run, but "often" and "in the long run" did not work for Phoebe. Why wait when most situations—for example, the contest favoring Deerfield—could be easily and immediately changed from unfair to fair by using math?

Math had always made sense to Phoebe: Rules were followed, formulas were applied, and answers came out right or wrong. Both sides of the equation were equal, and equal was fair. Right now the equation between Granville and

Deerfield was unequal because Deerfield had two huge sales on its side while Granville had zero. And, as in math, the solution was simple: Make both sides even by giving each school one huge sale. Then the contest could carry on, even and fair, the way it should be.

"Little sales like that won't add up enough," Phoebe snapped, giving up on trying to be patient.

"They might," Evan said hopefully, knitting his green-gloved fingers together.

Evan was really turning out to be a negative factor because all you needed was simple addition to know that in this case the small individual sales would *never* add up to two huge business sales.

"If you can't handle it, I'll just take care of this myself," Phoebe said, pulling on her scarf again as it came loose in a particularly chilly gust of wind. "I don't even really need a co-captain if you're not interested in helping Granville win." Big sales went faster with two people, so she wanted Evan's help, but at this point, it was becoming obvious she'd be better off on her own.

"It's not that I don't want to win—" Evan said.

Phoebe was about to ditch Evan once and for all when he suddenly looked over her shoulder and gasped loudly.

Phoebe jumped and looked around, ready for whatever

had shaken Evan. But there was nothing out of the ordinary on Blossom, just a man going into the flower store and a few bundled-up people heading toward their cars, bags of whatever they had purchased on their arms. There were also two kids walking down the sidewalk toward them. Phoebe didn't recognize them, which meant they were probably students at Deerfield. Was it the two of them who had caused such a severe reaction from Evan? He was frowning and his fists were clenched.

"Hey, Evan," the boy said. He had messy black hair and wore a Steelers jacket.

"Hey, Gabe," Evan said with a nod.

"It's nice to see you, Evan," the girl added. Her long brown hair was pulled back in a complicated braid tucked beneath a pair of bright pink earmuffs. Her words were perfectly nice, but Evan looked as though she'd just cursed him with an evil spell.

"Julie," he said, his voice curt—much curter than it had been when he greeted Gabe.

Why was easygoing Evan suddenly so on edge? Had this girl done something to him? Phoebe couldn't help herself— she stepped close to him in case he needed support. Gabe also looked a little confused by the situation.

"I haven't seen you since camp this summer," Julie went on, sounding genuinely pleased to see him.

Now Evan was glaring at Julie like she had said something awful, and Julie bit her lip.

"I really didn't mean—" Julie began, but Evan interrupted quickly.

"I don't want to talk about it," he said shortly. "I told you that a million times."

Wow, what had happened at this camp? Phoebe definitely wanted to know the entire story because whatever it was, it had brought out a whole new side of Evan—an angry side Phoebe would not have imagined existed.

"Well, we miss you on debate," Julie said, clearly trying to change the subject. "We're actually ranked number one in the state for the first time in the school's history if you can believe it," she told Evan, now sounding proud. But then she caught herself again. "I'm sure we'd be doing even better if you were still on the team, though."

"Really?" Evan said in a tone frostier than the cold wind blowing down Blossom. "Is there something better than being number one?"

"You know what I mean," Julie said, now sounding impatient.

It was obvious from his expression that Evan did not know. Phoebe was now officially dying to know what had happened between Julie and Evan.

"Well, Gabe and I should get going," Julie said, and Gabe nodded. "They're waiting for us at the hospital to buy Fantastic Five bars. We're the co-captains of the Deerfield sales team." They both stood just a little straighter at this. "I hope you guys are ready because Deerfield is going to blow you out of the water this year." She smiled like this was funny.

Phoebe drew in a breath, but there was no need to speak because Evan, whose cheeks were now turning an alarming shade of bright purple, beat her to it. "Well, Phoebe and I are the co-captains of the Granville team and we . . . have a few surprises for you."

Phoebe's eyebrows shot up. Did that mean what she thought it did?

Gabe grinned. "Bring it on," he said in a taunting tone. "But there's no way you're going to beat us."

Without another word, he and Julie sauntered off.

"What was *that* about?" Phoebe asked, turning to Evan.

But Evan didn't seem to have heard Phoebe. He was staring after Julie, his eyes narrowed. "I didn't know Julie was co-captain of Deerfield," he muttered. "But I should have guessed she'd get elected."

Evan punched his fist into his hand.

"She's not going to win," he said firmly, his tentative

tone long gone. "Phoebe, you were right. We're going to level the playing field. That sale at the town hall should be ours, and we're going to take it."

Now he was talking.

"It's the fair thing to do," Phoebe said, a grin stretching across her face. She could barely believe her luck. What a wonderful coincidence that they had run into Julie and Gabe!

They finally had a chance at winning the Challenge.

End of Day Sales Tally: Granville 96, Deerfield 71

CHAPTER 4

TUESDAY, DAY 2

Just before the final bell rang the loudspeaker at Deerfield Elementary let out a loud squawk, causing everyone in Julie's class to cover their ears. A few girls even shrieked.

"All right, folks, just wanted to remind everyone that our Chocolate Challenge is on," Principal Martin said in her usual cheery voice. "Be sure to pick up your sales sheets to sell those scrumptious Fantastic Five chocolate bars if you haven't already. Go, Team Deerfield!"

At least half the class was smiling at Julie, and a few pumped their fists.

"I know you're going to lead us to victory," Ms. Dunbar said.

Julie tried to look modest, but it was kind of hard. She

and Gabe had had a record sale at the hospital the day before: fifty-four boxes. They'd been there most of the afternoon, but a number like that was worth it. And today they'd go to the town hall and probably top their record. Julie couldn't wait.

But just then Julie noticed Amber Bates glaring at her. When Amber saw she had Julie's attention, she leaned over to her best friend, Fatima, and whispered, "She's such a goody-goody," just loudly enough for Julie to hear.

And just like that Julie's insides were quaking like the vanilla pudding she'd eaten at lunch. Julie knew that Amber had really wanted to be co-captain of the Deerfield sales team. Amber's older sister had been co-captain three years ago, so apparently it meant a lot to Amber. But it wasn't like Julie had intended to upset Amber—it wasn't her fault that more people had voted for her! Though clearly Amber thought it was.

Julie had always been proud of the things she excelled at, but this year, that had gotten complicated. People like Amber acted like doing well was some kind of crime, as if Julie studied and practiced and tried hard just to make them look bad. But Julie worked hard because she *enjoyed* doing well. It didn't make her a goody-goody, like she knew people said, did it?

She wished she could ignore Amber and keep feeling excited about the chocolate sale. Instead, her insides had turned sour with shame.

The final bell rang, and everyone raced for the door of the classroom.

"Slowly, people," Ms. Dunbar called, but it was a lost cause. It had snowed last night, and Julie's classmates were eager to go sledding and wage snowball fights. And hopefully sell some chocolate.

"Did you get the extra forms?" Gabe asked, coming up behind Julie and startling her out of her thoughts.

"Yeah, I got them at lunch," Julie said, trying to put Amber and Fatima out of her mind. Hopefully once she led Deerfield to their record win in the Challenge, people would be *grateful* Julie was good at things. "It's awesome that we went through our whole supply yesterday."

"Yeah," Gabe said as they walked down the crowded hall, skillfully sidestepping a group of fourth graders already in their coats and running down the hall. "We're definitely going to break the sales record this year."

Julie smiled. She hadn't really known Gabe before this, but she liked how excited he got about winning. It made her feel better about her own eagerness to do well. They were a good team.

"I need to drop off my family's order at the office before we go to the town hall," he told Julie.

"S'mores?" Julie asked, remembering he had said the S'mores were his favorite of the Fantastic Five.

"Yeah." Gabe nodded. "I'll probably eat half of them on the way home."

Julie laughed as they walked into Deerfield headquarters, where a big group of fifth and sixth graders were waiting for the first Challenge update and their sale assignments in town.

"Okay, let's get started," Julie said immediately. They only had a few hours to sell bars, so they couldn't waste too much time talking.

The other students quieted quickly, ready to get down to business.

"As you know, Fur Friends Animal Sanctuary is our charity," Julie said.

"Who is Granville raising money for?" a fifth grader asked.

"I'm not sure," Julie said. It didn't really matter since Granville would lose.

Though the mention of Granville reminded Julie of the unfortunate run-in with Evan Black the day before. Julie got that quivery feeling again, remembering the way Evan had glared at her. She really hadn't meant to embarrass him at the day camp they'd both attended that summer. And she'd been hoping that after all these months he'd have gotten over it. Or at least forgiven her.

"It should be posted on their website," Gabe said, interrupting Julie's unwelcome thoughts.

"I'll look it up," Eva Santiago volunteered, heading over to a computer.

"Yesterday we got some good numbers at Village Pizza and East Wind Books in addition to the big sale at the hospital," Julie said while Eva waited for the computer to fire up, checking both businesses off on the spreadsheet that listed every business on their side of town. "We're off to a strong start—seventy-one boxes so far. Today Gabe and I will go to the town hall to lock that in. It will probably be our single biggest sale!"

"Woo-hoo!" a fifth grader cheered, while several other kids pumped their fists.

Julie was excited to take on the town hall sale. Last year Ian Watson and Evan had made a record sale of fifty-nine boxes that Julie wanted to break. Though would it make Evan even angrier at her? Probably. Ugh, there was the quivery feeling again.

"Granville chose the community center for its charity," Eva announced.

"Our charity is way better!" Gabe cheered.

"And I'll check their sales numbers too—" Eva sucked in her breath in a long whistle. Everyone in the room turned to look at her. "No way."

"What is it?" Julie demanded. She hurried over and peered at the screen. "They've already sold ninety-six boxes?!"

How was it possible that Granville was ahead of Deerfield after the very first day? That had never, ever happened before.

"That's high for first-day sales?" Gabe asked. Julie didn't know how he could be so clueless.

"Yes," Julie said. "It's incredibly high—I've never seen first-day numbers like that from Granville."

"Sounds like they're inflating the score," Gabe said sharply. His eyes were flashing, and his face was tense. "I'm going to make some calls and see what's going on." He strode out of the room to get his phone and use it outside—even after-school phone use was not permitted inside the building.

Was Gabe overreacting? Had Granville just worked super hard on the first day? Or was something funny going on? Julie realized she was standing there gaping after him. She pulled herself together. "Don't worry," she said, turning back to the group. "We'll figure out what their strategy was. And our sales numbers will go way up once we go to the town hall." She smiled confidently. "Now let's figure out where you guys should go to sell chocolate this afternoon."

After she instructed people where to make their sales and marked it down on their spreadsheet, she straightened the piles of forms and tried not to get too antsy. Where was Gabe? They really needed to get to the town hall and make that sale if they were going to catch up.

A few more students came in to get sales sheets. Just as Julie handed over the last one, Gabe stomped into the room. His eyes were blazing, and his hands were clenched into fists.

"Granville!" he shouted. "They cheated!"

Julie gasped. It couldn't be possible—could it? Evan might hold a grudge, but he wasn't a cheater.

Was he? Had he done this to get back at her?

Gabe kicked a chair, and Julie saw a second grader cowering behind the sales table. "Gabe, are you sure?" she asked.

"I'm positive." Gabe said, glowering "They sold in *our* territory. At the town hall! They took our biggest sale!"

CHAPTER 5
TUESDAY, DAY 2

Gabe was so furious it was hard to breathe.

Granville had cheated. Cheated! Gabe was fighting mad.

Julie started saying something about speaking to Mr. Ryan, their faculty advisor, but Gabe cut her off. "If this is how Granville wants to play it, I say we show them how it's done," Gabe said angrily. Julie took a hasty step backward. Had he shouted? "They took our biggest sale, so let's take theirs. Let's go sell our chocolate at the police and fire station."

"We can't cheat," Julie said weakly.

Was she kidding? He knew Julie's reputation—she liked to be number one. Well, if she wanted to get in the lead, they'd have to meet Granville on their own level.

"They started it," he said, possibly more sharply than he'd intended because Julie took another step back. "We can't let them get away with it."

Julie bit her lip for a moment, and Gabe waited, hoping she had seen reason. "Cheating's . . . wrong," she said finally.

Gabe felt like his head might explode. "I know," he said as calmly as he could. "And I never would have suggested it. I always play by the rules."

Julie looked reassured by this.

"But," Gabe continued, "the way it works in sports is that if the other team cheats, you get a freebie."

"A freebie?" Julie asked uncertainly.

"Yeah, it's like a free pass," Gabe explained. He decided not to mention that this theory of sportsmanship came from the Gabe Menendez playbook and not something more official. But they were not in this to be wimps. Granville had cheated, which meant they'd practically asked for payback. "They took one sale from us, so they owe us a sale on their side of town."

Julie was still biting her lip, but she nodded slowly. "I guess I see what you mean," she said. "But I really think it makes more sense to tell a teacher. That way they can tell us where we should go for our freebie."

Gabe tried not to roll his eyes. He had heard people call

Julie a goody-goody, and now he could see why. But as his co-captain, he needed her on board. "I think we should just take care of it ourselves," Gabe said. "The teachers don't want us going to them for every little thing."

Julie did not look convinced.

"Look," Gabe said, trying another tactic. "What do you think happens if we do nothing and then Deerfield loses the Challenge for the first time ever? People will be really angry at us."

Julie was suddenly blinking a lot, and Gabe realized he'd finally hit a nerve. "They'll think we're wimps," he said. And then it came to him, the thing he could say to get Julie on his side. "They'll call us goody-goodies."

Julie drew in a sharp breath. "Yeah, you're right," she whispered.

Gabe wanted to cheer, but he kept himself together and just nodded seriously. "And if it gets out that we knew they cheated and we didn't do anything about it . . ." He let his voice trail off so that Julie would imagine the worst—after all, it would be a disaster if they let that happen.

"So we should just make the police and fire station our freebie," Julie said, like she was trying to talk herself into it.

"Yup," Gabe said, happy to help. "It's just taking what now belongs to us—like a swap—one good sale for another good sale."

"It makes sense when you say it like that," Julie said. "I mean, really it's not even cheating."

"Not at all," Gabe said, grinning. "Not at all."

There was an icy wind blowing as they stood on their side—the east side—of Blossom Boulevard. After the stuffy heat of the school and the anger that had burned in Gabe's belly at the news of Granville's underhandedness, it felt good.

"Are we really doing this?" Julie asked, shifting from one foot to the other.

They were at the northeast corner of Blossom Boulevard and Walnut Drive. Hazel Avenue, where the big police and fire station was located, was one block west. Once they crossed Blossom Boulevard heading that way, they would officially be in Granville's territory.

Gabe nodded. "It's game time," he said, then looked both ways and crossed the street.

CHAPTER 6

TUESDAY, DAY 2

"Thanks so much," Phoebe said, smiling at Mrs. Crenshaw, the owner of Treasure Chest Antiques. She was also the co-chair of the Granville PTA, so she had splurged on five boxes.

"My pleasure," Mrs. Crenshaw said. "I like to use the bars as stocking stuffers for my grandkids. And I save plenty for myself, of course." She'd selected two boxes of Toffee Crunch, a dark chocolate bar stuffed with big chunks of buttery toffee, and three of the Triple Crown.

The small store smelled like rose petals and was crowded with old vases, knickknacks, dishes, and paintings. Scared of knocking something over, Phoebe was trying to stand very, very still while making the sale, but the counter held a glass bowl filled with old jewelry that she couldn't help admiring. Phoebe gently touched a gold ring with a large black stone.

Mrs. Crenshaw grinned. "Open it up," she said.

Phoebe was confused. "The ring?" she asked. She was not aware that jewelry could open.

But Mrs. Crenshaw nodded, so Phoebe picked up the ring and pulled at it. The stone swung to one side, revealing a small, empty chamber. "Cool," she said, impressed.

"In the olden days, people would wear them and hide poison inside," Mrs. Crenshaw said. "Then, at a banquet, they would sneak to their archenemy's plate and sprinkle the poison onto their food."

Phoebe was fascinated. "Really?" she asked.

Mrs. Crenshaw grinned. "Yup—good thing the rivalry between Granville and Deerfield is a friendly one, right? You wouldn't want any enemies trying to off you by sprinkling poison onto your chocolate bar."

"No," Phoebe agreed, happy that this year the rivalry wasn't just friendly but was finally fair too. She carefully put the poison ring back into the glass bowl. "Thanks again, Mrs. Crenshaw," Phoebe said. "Enjoy the chocolate!" She pushed the glass door, heading back into the cold, where Evan was waiting for her.

He'd gone to Stop the Press, the newspaper shop that

also sold snacks, drinks, and lottery tickets, to make his own sale but had finished before her. "How'd you do?" he asked.

"Five boxes," she reported, pulling on her gloves.

"Nice," Evan said. "I only sold two boxes, but since they sell candy there themselves, I figure that's pretty good. And I ran into some fifth graders who sold four boxes at the Craft Bizarre."

"Great," Phoebe said, adding up the numbers in her head. That would get them to 107—and she was expecting a massive sale at their next stop. Hopefully they'd still be in the lead.

"Is it time for us to go back to the police and fire station?" Evan asked. His face was pink from the arctic wind.

Phoebe pulled her phone out of her pocket to check. It took two tries because it kept sliding out of her gloved hands. They had gone to the station the moment the final bell of the school day rang, but Chief Wahid was on his break, so they'd been told to return after 3:30. Phoebe finally managed to punch the button with her gloved finger—it was now almost four.

"Yeah, let's go," Phoebe said. "And let's see if we can get them to buy even more boxes than we sold them last year."

"They bought thirty-five boxes last year?" Evan asked.

"Thirty-seven," Phoebe corrected. "Let's get that up to at least forty!" That would probably be a good enough margin to keep Granville in the lead.

"I was thinking," Evan said as they turned on Hazel Avenue. "We should start by saying something about the Police and Firemen's Holiday Pancake Breakfast, like how it's a really important tradition that they make happen for our town every year."

Phoebe grinned, knowing just what he was thinking before he could say it. "And then we say another great town tradition is our Chocolate Challenge and how much we appreciate them helping us out with that."

Evan nodded happily. "Exactly," he said.

Yes, they were in sync, and Phoebe was loving it. Initially, when Evan balked at finally making the Challenge fair by taking the town hall sale, Phoebe had not been sure he was up to the task of co-captain. But ever since they'd run into Julie and Gabe, Evan had been the best co-captain imaginable. This reminded Phoebe of the tension between Julie and Evan—she really wanted to know that story— but now, with a major sale pending, was not the time to get into it.

Phoebe straightened her scarf as they walked into the big lobby that functioned as the front desk for both official departments. Photos of the police force dotted one wall, while the members of the fire department covered the other. Because the stations served Scottsdale, the surrounding farmland, and the three other towns nearby, it was big, with a lot of employees. Hungry, chocolate-loving employees.

"Hi, Sergeant Applegate," Phoebe said in her most professional voice to the officer seated behind the tall counter. The room bustled as officers strode past, their shoes clicking on the hardwood floor. "We're back to see both the police and fire chiefs about the Chocolate Challenge."

She was about to pull her sales sheets out of her bag to start taking down their order—their huge order—when she realized Sergeant Applegate's forehead had scrunched up. "I think there must be a mistake," he said slowly.

Phoebe's hand froze over her bag. "What do you mean?" she asked.

"Well, two students were just here selling chocolate bars," Sergeant Applegate said. "Sorry, Phoebe. They already took everyone's orders. Were you supposed to be with them?"

An iciness much colder than the coldest day in Scottsdale was suddenly creeping through Phoebe's veins. "These students," she began, "were they students at Granville?" If they were overeager Granville students who had swooped in for her sale, Phoebe would be annoyed but forgiving.

But if it wasn't Granville students who had made this sale, this *record* sale, then—

"I'm not sure," Sergeant Applegate said. "They didn't say."

"What did they look like?" Phoebe asked.

"I can't really recall," said Sergeant Applegate. Phoebe could not help feeling that this made him quite bad at his job. What kind of police officer neglected to notice details of a potential criminal? Not that they could be sure a crime had happened, not before they had all the facts. But shouldn't an officer be alert just in case?

"Oh, but their names were Julie and Gabe, if that helps," Sergeant Applegate said, completely unaware that he had basically allowed two criminals to escape.

Phoebe had to bite her lip from saying something inappropriate as Evan politely thanked Sergeant Applegate and dragged her outside. Once she was on the sidewalk, Phoebe kicked the nearest non-human object, which was a bike rack. It hurt but not as much as the knowledge that once again the Challenge was completely and totally unfair.

"I can't believe they did this," Phoebe raged.

"Me neither," Evan said, shaking his head. "It's not the kind of thing Julie would ever do. She *always* follows the rules—that's why people sometimes call her a goody-goody."

"Well, now they can call her a hypocrite because that's

what she is," Phoebe said. She considered kicking the bike rack again. "Because she just totally broke the rules. And we can't let Deerfield get away with it."

She looked at Evan to see if he was willing to do what it would take to keep this contest even on both sides of the equation. And to her relief, Evan was nodding.

"What is their next biggest sale?" Phoebe asked. "Because whatever it is, it's ours now."

But now Evan was shaking his head. Maybe he didn't have what it took after all.

"I don't think we should take their next sale," he said as they started walking. Phoebe's fingers were nearly numb, and she pulled out her gloves to warm them.

"Why not?" she asked. It seemed obvious that if Deerfield took one of their sales, Granville should take one of Deerfield's, to even things out.

"Because we already did that and it didn't work," he said. "I mean, we made things fair when we took one of the town's two biggest sales, letting them have the other. But they actually cheated when they took this sale. And I don't think it's enough to just take another sale from them. They'll do it too! We need to do something different—otherwise they'll just keep cheating and they'll beat us."

Phoebe was deeply impressed by Evan's evaluation of the situation—and his strategy of introducing a variable to the equation. He was right: Simply making the equation equal with a known factor—taking another sale in Deerfield territory—wasn't going to work if Deerfield responded by making it unequal again. But introducing an unknown quantity—an x—would change the equation itself. And since Deerfield had made the choice to cheat, why should Granville follow the rules? *That* would not be fair.

"I'm with you," she said as they reached the corner of Birch and Hazel. "What do you have in mind?"

"Well, I'm a prank expert," Evan said slowly. "At least I used to be. And I can tell you firsthand that a well-crafted prank can totally mess up something as delicate as a chocolate sale."

And now Phoebe was intrigued. Very intrigued. "Tell me more," she said.

End of Day Sales Tally: Granville 107, Deerfield 99

CHAPTER 7

SATURDAY, DAY 6

Julie's feet were starting to freeze, and her nose was icy.

"How much farther do you think it is?" Gabe asked her. They were walking down Route 28, the small highway that led out of town, and after trekking for over an hour, they were definitely outside of town. They were surrounded by snowy farmland dotted with houses and barns and wide fields, pristine and sparkling in the midday sun. It had been pretty at first, but now the glare from the sun shining on the white snow was hurting Julie's eyes. It didn't help that her muscles ached from the six boxes of Fantastic Five chocolate bars she was carrying, a bag with three boxes slung over each shoulder.

"I don't know," Julie said. "I feel like we should have come to it already."

"Me too," Gabe said. He shifted the bag on his left shoulder. "Mr. Edwards said he was in this big rush to get the chocolate, but he couldn't just go pick it up himself yesterday?"

"I know, it's weird," Julie agreed.

The small typed note on school stationery had been left in their classroom headquarters on Friday. It explained that Walter Edwards had placed a large rush order of chocolate and asked if someone from the team could deliver it the next day. It was a major pain to walk the boxes all the way out there, but Julie figured it was a great bonus that the order had come in at all.

"I wish I'd asked my parents to drive us," she added. "I didn't realize it was so far." In fact, the note had made it sound like it was a ten-minute walk, tops.

"Yeah, me too," Gabe said, shifting one of his bags.

"It'll be worth it for the sale," Julie said, deciding to stay optimistic despite the fact that her shoulders felt like they were about to fall off. "Twelve boxes for one home is awesome. Maybe when he sees how cold and wet we are, he'll feel bad for us and we can talk him into buying a few more."

"Yeah, I'll use my wet socks to get a sale!" Gabe said. "But he has to come pick the chocolate up himself this time."

"Seriously," Julie agreed, her boot crunching down on a chunk of icy snow. "Did you see that we pulled ahead of Granville in sales?"

"Not by much, though," Gabe said. A pickup truck was driving by, and it slowed as it passed them, careful to give them wide berth. "We have to sell everywhere we can and *maximize* every sale we make." He grinned at her.

"Definitely," Julie said, grinning back. She liked that instead of staying annoyed about the whole "maximize" thing, Gabe had decided to turn it into a joke. Unlike *some* people Julie could think of who turned one mistake into a months-long grudgefest. Or called her a goody-goody just because she was good at school things like vocabulary words.

Working with Gabe was fun. Yes, he could get intense, but after Granville sold in their territory—something she still couldn't believe they'd done—she was glad he'd been there with his advice about how to handle things. Julie didn't play sports, so she hadn't known that it was acceptable to take a freebie. She was glad all that was behind them now, though—each team had taken their freebie and now it was time to play by the rules. Exactly how Julie liked it.

Just then she saw the mailbox they were looking for. "That's it!" she cried, pointing to the snow-covered red metal box with the name "Edwards" written on the side in block letters.

Gabe's brow wrinkled as they got closer. "It looks kind of old," he said.

It did—the sides were coated with rust and the flag hung off at an odd angle.

"Maybe they haven't gotten around to fixing it," Julie said uncertainly. Because truthfully it didn't just look broken or old—it looked like it hadn't been used in eons.

"Maybe," Gabe said.

Julie glanced toward the farm, but tall trees blocked her from getting a proper view of the house and barn.

"The driveway hasn't been plowed," Gabe said, an edge creeping into his voice.

He was right—there was no way a car could get up to the house. But perhaps that explained why Mr. Edwards hadn't come to pick up the chocolate himself. "Maybe he can't drive," she said. "So he had no way to get into town. "And look—I see footprints going up to the house. Someone's been here recently."

Julie felt warmer already. Maybe Mr. Edwards had walked down to the road to see if Julie and Gabe were there yet. Maybe he was heating up some apple cider for them right now as a thank-you for their long walk. She smiled, thinking of how they would make this old man's day by coming all the way out here to hand-deliver his favorite chocolate.

Gabe didn't seem to have the same vision, and he was muttering under his breath as they staggered through the foot of snow, slipping a little as they went. At one point, Julie almost dropped a bag of chocolate but managed to save it by landing hard on one knee.

Meanwhile, Gabe was pushing his way through the snow as fast as he could. And when he passed the line of trees, he let out a shout. "I knew it!"

Julie struggled to her feet and hurried to catch up with him.

The view that revealed itself to her when she passed the pine trees was a depressing one. The farmhouse was long abandoned: The porch and walkway were covered with snow, the windows were dirty and dark, and just in case there was any hope left, the roof was partially caved in.

"We came all this way for nothing," Gabe shouted, throwing his bags down in a snowdrift.

But just then Julie caught sight of something, a bit of color on the door. She made her way along the path and up the steps.

"What is it?" Gabe called, hurrying toward her.

"A Post-it," Julie said, leaning in to read it.

"GOT YOU," it said in big, bold letters.

Well, that explained the footprints—someone had walked up the snowy drive of this abandoned house to leave a mean note for Julie and Gabe. And with a sick feeling in her stomach, Julie realized she knew just who would do this.

"Granville!" Gabe cried, slapping the doorjamb above the note.

Julie wanted so badly to have another culprit, or at least the possibility of one—she did not want to wade back into the murky, unsettling waters of a contest without rules for a second time. But of course he was right, of course it was Evan Black, prank king of Granville, because who else could it be?

"We gave them a shot at playing fair," Gabe said, his voice scorched with anger. "And what did they do? They tricked us into coming all this way for nothing. They *pranked* us."

"Maybe—" Julie began.

"Evan and his stupid pranks," Gabe said, shaking his head. He'd actually appreciated the pranks when Evan was a student at Deerfield but not anymore. "You know what this means, right? It means we have to come up with a way to prank them back."

Julie did not want to be having this conversation. She did not want to be standing in a snowdrift, feeling melted snow slide into her boot, her knee throbbing from her fall, stuck miles outside of town while Gabe had a meltdown. And most of all she did not want to be talking about stupid, time-wasting pranks. This wasn't how Julie did things.

"I really think we should just follow the rules," she said in a small voice.

Gabe looked at her evenly. "What rules?" he asked. "Do you see any rules here?" He swept his arm around, and for a moment, Julie took in the total silence of the abandoned landscape. Even in the bright sunshine, the rotting farmhouse and empty land looked spooky. "Anyway, it's not like the teachers hand out a guidebook that says you can't prank someone during the contest."

"Well, yeah, but that's because they assume everyone knows you shouldn't do that," Julie said, feeling that this was obvious.

"Everyone but Granville, apparently," Gabe said. "And if we let them get away with this, we'll lose. We have to prank them back."

"Maybe there's something else we can do," Julie said. "Like go to Mr. Ryan."

But as soon as she said it, Julie knew there was no going to the teacher in charge of the Challenge. Because that's what goody-goodies did, and Julie would not be a goody-goody. Thanks to Granville and their stupid pranks, there was no other choice. Deerfield *had* to come up with a prank of their own.

"Okay," Julie said, ignoring the fact that while she knew this was their best option, there was a tiny prickle of doubt poking insistently at the back of her mind. "We have a long walk back. Let's use it to make a plan."

CHAPTER 8

SATURDAY, DAY 6

"I have some news," Gabe's dad announced that night at dinner. "Good news."

Gabe looked up eagerly. Was it possible that his dad had finally realized how much the family needed a new Xbox? Too bad his brother, David, was out at a friend's, so they wouldn't get to break it in together.

"I'm up for a promotion at work," his dad said, smiling.

Gabe tried to look happy for his dad even though this was not the good news Gabe had hoped for. "Wonderful," Gabe's mom said, leaning over to plant a loud kiss on his dad's cheek. His mom was a kindergarten teacher and tended to be very encouraging about pretty much everything.

"How's the chocolate sale going, sweetie?" his mom asked, scooping up a steamy helping of the mac and cheese Gabe's dad had made for dinner that night and delivering it to Gabe's plate.

"Great," Gabe said quickly. "Very non-competitive."

His mother looked a little confused. Had he overdone it?

"It's been fun working with Julie," Gabe kept talking quickly, in case damage control was needed. "We're a good team." He knew his parents and coaches had been worried about his team-building skills. Sure enough, his mom smiled at this.

"Wonderful," she said. "Julie's the girl who was awarded that merit scholarship for a robotics camp, wasn't she? I remember there was an article about her in the paper this summer."

"Yes, that's her," Gabe said, taking a big bite of the creamy mac and cheese. He had no idea if Julie had won the scholarship, but it sounded right. And hadn't she said something about a camp to Evan when they ran into him?

"I'm sure Julie will be a wonderful influence," his mom said approvingly.

Gabe tried not to roll his eyes. He was the one who had been a good influence on Julie when he pointed out that they had to prank Granville back or lose the contest—not that he could tell his mom that of course.

"I'm sure she will," Gabe said. Though so far in their quest to come up with a prank, she had been no use at all. Unfortunately, neither had Gabe.

He had come up with some good ideas, like dressing up as zombies and jumping out from behind bushes as Granville students were going to sell chocolate, then grabbing their boxes and running away, but Julie had pointed out that that might be illegal. They also didn't have zombie costumes.

"We're pleased to see you're being a team player," Gabe's dad said. "And remembering that there's more to life than winning."

For a second time, Gabe had to work not to roll his eyes.

"Oh, and I was able to reschedule your dentist appointment," Gabe's mom said. "So you can go sell chocolate after school on Thursday instead of getting your checkup. The dentist said it's fine to go in a few weeks, when the contest is over." Then her brows scrunched as she looked at Gabe. "Sweetie, are you okay?"

Gabe was more than okay—he was electrified! And that was because his mom had just given him an idea for the perfect prank to pull on Granville!

End of Day Sales Tally: Granville 168, Deerfield 162

CHAPTER 9

MONDAY, DAY 8

"We've been waiting for you!" the bank clerk said to Evan, grinning at him from behind the counter.

Evan glanced at her nameplate, then grinned right back, sales sheets in hand, pen ready. "Sorry it took us a bit to get here, Ms. Hansen—we've had a record number of sales this year." This probably wasn't true, but it sounded good.

"Well, we're about to add to that," Ms. Hansen said, standing up and smoothing her pants. "A few of us have decided to make Fantastic Five baskets for our friends and family as our holiday gifts. So I hope you're ready for a massive order."

Evan wouldn't have thought he could smile any bigger,

but it turned out he could. A massive order of Fantastic Five bars sounded, well, fantastic!

"Let me gather everyone up," Ms. Hansen said. "Claude, can you handle any customers so the rest of us can start placing our chocolate orders?" she said to the man at the next desk.

"Yes, as long as you don't leave without taking my order too," Claude said, winking at Evan.

"No, sir, I'd never do that," Evan said. He settled in the chair in front of Ms. Hansen's desk to wait for her return. The bank was small, but Evan knew there were at least ten workers in the back office—maybe even more. He put his sales sheets on the wooden desk so he'd be ready to start writing as soon as they came out. Sun shone through the big front windows, bathing the room in a gentle gold glow that Evan found relaxing.

The phone rang on Claude's desk. Evan glanced over and took note that his last name was Lafarge—Evan wanted to be able to thank everyone by name, a tip Phoebe had given him, along with saying "sir" and "ma'am." Evan missed Phoebe, but she had arranged to go to the Griddle, the local diner, where one of her neighbors worked, and it was a sale she could do alone, so it made sense for Evan to go solo today as well. And he was going to use it as his first opportunity to show off his skills as Evan "Sales King" Black.

It had been fun to spend a few hours playing the old role of prank king over the weekend—Evan had missed that. Plotting the fake sale to a farm in the middle of nowhere—well, it went so smoothly it was like he'd never given up pranks at all. The best part was imagining Julie's face when she saw the Post-it on the door. After all, it was her fault he'd had to stop pranking, so it was fitting that she would be the victim of his brief but glorious comeback. Really, after a prank like that, it was a shame he'd have to go back into retirement.

"Oh, I see," Mr. Lafarge was saying to the person on the phone in a serious voice. "Yes, I'll send him home right away."

Evan didn't want to eavesdrop, but it was impossible not to in the small space. He hoped that whoever had to go home would give his order to Evan before leaving.

"You're Evan, right?" Mr. Lafarge said, standing up and walking over to Evan.

"Yes, sir, I am," Evan said, sitting up straight.

"That was your mother on the phone," Mr. Lafarge said. "She called to remind you about your dentist appointment this afternoon. She said you're late, so you need to get home and meet her right away."

Evan stood up. He hadn't remembered he had an appointment. Such bad timing! "Okay, thanks," he said, stuffing the sales sheets in his bag.

And then he stopped. He did not have a dentist appointment this afternoon. His mom wasn't even at home. She was a nurse, and Mondays she didn't leave the clinic until 5:00. Evan looked at the clock on Ms. Hansen's desk. It was 3:37. Something was going on, and Evan had a pretty strong hunch it had nothing to do with his teeth and everything to do with the Challenge. As a former prank king, he was pretty good at recognizing a prank.

"The person who called," Evan began. "Did she—"

"Your mother's not angry," Mr. Lafarge interrupted. "But she was clear that you need to hurry."

"That's the thing," Evan said, squeezing his hands together. "I don't think it was my mom who called. I don't have an appointment!"

"I understand, son. No one likes the dentist," Mr. Lafarge said. He put his hand on the small of Evan's back and began steering Evan toward the door. "But best to just get it over with. And you don't want to keep your mother waiting."

"It wasn't her; I'm sure of it," Evan pleaded with Mr. Lafarge. But the bank clerk was surprisingly strong, and at this point he was nearly shoving Evan out the door.

"I promised her you'd leave right away, and at the Bank of Scottsdale, we always keep our word," Mr. Lafarge said firmly. He opened the door, letting in a blast of frigid air, and pushed Evan out into the cold. "Hustle now, son."

Evan stood outside the door of the bank, peering inside and hoping Ms. Hansen would appear. Perhaps he could convince her that the call had been a vicious prank. But she was still in back, and Mr. Lafarge made a shooing motion with his hands.

Evan gritted his teeth. There was no convincing Mr. Lafarge that the call had been a farce. He had to leave. His only hope was reaching Phoebe and getting her to the bank ASAP to get that massive sale.

As he grabbed his phone from his pocket, he admitted to himself that he'd been had—Deerfield had hit him with an oldie but goody, a prank that had stood the test of time and that, for today, had gotten the best of him.

But as he turned the corner, he realized something else. Deerfield had answered a prank with a prank, and there was only one way to respond to that: with another prank.

Which meant that Evan "Prank King" Black would have to come out of retirement one more time.

CHAPTER 10

MONDAY, DAY 8

"Is he gone?" Gabe asked, accidentally bumping Julie out of the way so he could peek around her and see the bank. The two of them were in the lobby of the movie theater across the street, and Gabe was giddy as they watched to see if the call Julie put through to the bank pretending to be Evan's mother had actually worked.

"He's arguing with the clerk . . . Now it looks like he's leaving. Wait, wait, he's still standing outside," Julie said, not taking her eyes off Evan. "Okay, he's walking now, and yes, he turned the corner. It worked!"

"Awesome!" Gabe said as he raised up his hand to high-five Julie, who slapped his palm with real strength.

Julie continually surprised him, but in a good way. For example, he had been concerned Julie would come up with some lame reason they shouldn't try to pull off Gabe's awesome idea. When they met up after the final bell that afternoon, she had seemed iffy about pranking Granville at all. And then, when they arrived at sales headquarters, Amber Bates had been discussing how Julie was too scared to do what it took to win, a conversation that had stopped abruptly when they walked in and a conversation that Gabe feared was true. But instead, when he presented the fake calling plan to a small group of trusted volunteers, Julie had been the first one to get on board, even offering to make the call and doing a pretty convincing job of it.

"This calls for some chocolate," Gabe said now. He'd gotten his allowance and had two S'more bars in his backpack, the perfect way to celebrate. He could already taste the crunchy graham cracker chunks and fluffed marshmallow core.

"Let's wait," Julie said, all business. "Evan took his phone out as he was leaving, so we should get in there fast. We don't want anyone from Granville coming while we're in the middle of getting the sale."

It was an excellent point. They'd celebrate once the sale was theirs.

Gabe and Julie hurried into the bank, where workers stood grouped around the front desk, pretty much waiting for them to arrive.

"Hi, our friend Evan asked us to come by and take your orders," Gabe said smoothly.

"Oh, wonderful," a woman said, smiling. "We were hoping he'd send someone. We didn't want to miss our chance to order!"

"He sent two of us," Gabe said grandly, gesturing to Julie. "And we're both ready to get everyone stocked up on chocolate."

Ten minutes later, they were out the door. They'd sold fourteen boxes of chocolate, which was awesome, but the icing on the sale was that it was fourteen boxes that they'd taken from Granville.

Score one—a big one—for Deerfield!

Now it was time to celebrate!

End of Day Sales Tally: Granville 172, Deerfield 184

CHAPTER 11

TUESDAY, DAY 9

"Is it true that Deerfield is starting some kind of war with us over the Chocolate Challenge?" Roy Butler asked Phoebe. The final bell had just rung, and the halls were filling up with students, most of whom were talking about what had taken place yesterday afternoon.

"No," Phoebe said, but then reconsidered. "Well, actually, yeah, it's a prank war, but don't worry, it's not a war they can win."

"Glad to hear it," Roy said, holding up his hand to high-five Phoebe. "Granville rules!"

A few nearby students cheered at that.

"If you want Granville to win, come get a sales sheet," Rosita Perez said, coming up to them.

Phoebe realized that she, as co-captain, should have been the one to say that to Roy. She was so focused on plotting out their next prank against Deerfield that she'd forgotten to push sales.

"Yeah, you should," she called to Roy, who was already melting into a crowd of flag football players headed to practice.

"I'll make sure to give him a sales sheet tomorrow," Phoebe told Rosita as they headed to sales headquarters. She made a mental note to start carrying sheets with her to class—every sale counted, especially after what had happened the day before.

Just thinking about the prank Deerfield had pulled on Evan had Phoebe fuming: The bank sale would have been a great addition to their lead, and Deerfield had snatched it from them, along with the top score of the day. And even worse, Deerfield had done it by using Granville's strategy— yet again! Deerfield had done nothing but copy Phoebe and Evan, when all they'd wanted was to have a fair shot.

Of course Phoebe wished that it had not come to this. She had been invested in a fair contest, but Deerfield had gone and ruined that, continuing to push for the advantage. Really they were forcing Granville to introduce new and more powerful variables because it was the only way to keep things fair.

So, yes, this was now a war.

But as Phoebe had assured Roy, she was confident victory would be theirs. Between Evan's pranking skills and Phoebe's strategic planning, there was no way they could lose.

Phoebe inhaled deeply as she walked into sales head-quarters. The room had started to smell like the boxes of Fantastic Five that were stacked against the back wall, a rich chocolate scent. Truly nothing in the world smelled as good as Fantastic Five bars.

The room was crowded, and Phoebe hurried over to help Evan hand out sales sheets and assign places to sell while Rosita joined up with a few of her friends and then headed out to sell boxes.

"I've got this, but can you grab some extra sales sheets?" Evan asked after a few minutes. Their supply was running low.

"Sure," Phoebe said. But before going to the back closet, she made a quick stop at their chocolate supply. Phoebe had just gotten her allowance, so she took two Fantastic Five bars: a Sweet and Simple for Evan, which she passed him, and a Lava bar for herself. She opened her bar and took a big bite, then closed her eyes to savor the silky milk chocolate and velvety caramel core. The Lava bar was complete perfection.

Then she grabbed the sales sheets and got back to work.

"As soon as everyone's gone, we can figure out our next move," Phoebe told Evan in a low voice as she passed a sales sheet to a boy from her English class.

"Actually, I already have an idea, but we're going to need some help with it," Evan said softly. "Who do you think we should ask?"

Phoebe was once again reminded that Evan was the new kid in school. "What are we looking for?" she asked him.

"Someone stealth," he said. "Who can do sneaky things under the radar."

Phoebe did not know anyone like that—this was a school, not a recruitment center for the CIA. "Well, maybe—" she began.

"I can help," a girl said right behind them, making Phoebe jump and Evan nearly drop the sales sheet he was holding.

Phoebe turned and saw it was Avery Wagner, a short girl with long black hair who was in a few of her classes and who was also apparently quite stealth since neither Phoebe nor Evan had heard her come up behind them.

"Great," Evan said. "You're hired."

A few moments later, the room had cleared, leaving Avery, Phoebe, and Evan behind. Phoebe closed the door firmly—they did not need anyone sneaking in during this conversation. Then she sat down at the desk across from Evan.

"What do you need me to do?" Avery asked, folding her hands in her lap. "My cousin goes to Deerfield, and I am sick and tired of hearing him gloat about how we always lose. I'll do whatever it takes to get us a win this year."

Phoebe nodded, appreciating Avery's attitude. In the face of how unfair the entire Challenge had become, it was important to have strong factors like Avery on their side.

"I have something," Evan said. "Something that will sabotage a sale, and I need you to give it to Julie."

"Or Gabe?" Avery asked.

Evan shook his head. "No, it has to be Julie," he said.

Phoebe was suddenly reminded of the mysterious grudge Evan held against Julie, but of course now was not the time to ask after it, not in the middle of a planning session.

"Why?" Avery asked.

"I don't know Gabe that well," Evan said. "But I know Julie, and trust me, this will get her off her game in a major way."

"What is it?" Phoebe asked, leaning forward eagerly.

But Evan was busy spreading out a map of Scottsdale on the table between them.

"I have it from a Deerfield source that tomorrow Julie is doing a sale at Dandelion Day Care, on Laurel and Spruce," he said, pointing on the map. "And there are at least two other volunteers going with her because she has to bring the order there."

Phoebe was impressed that Evan was using his old connections to Deerfield so effectively.

"We have to give this to Julie in the middle of the sale, when she's inside," Evan went on. "I'm wondering if you could somehow hide in the yard and then follow her into the day care."

And now Phoebe was no longer impressed with Evan's skills. It was a good thing she was here to offer a strategy that would actually be effective. After all, what respectable day care allowed elementary school students to just hang out in their yard for no reason?

"I think it would work better if Avery waited for Julie here, at the Mocha Bean," Phoebe said, putting her finger on the spot where the small café was located, two blocks away from the day care. "That way she can see when Julie goes by and tag along with the students who are helping her."

"Won't Julie notice I didn't walk out of school with them?" Avery asked. "And wonder why some girl they don't know is suddenly joining them?"

Phoebe shook her head. "I can't be sure, but I don't think so," she said, ready to prove this with facts. "Julie is one of those people who's really focused on her goals and people like that miss a lot of what's going on around them."

Now it was Evan's turn to look impressed. "Yeah, that's totally how she is—how'd you know that?" he asked.

Phoebe tried to look modest. "I pick up on things," she said. Math was about details and so was Phoebe. "I think if you just act like you were late leaving school but now you're there to help them, she'll just think you're a random fifth grader and not question it."

"And if she accepts it, the others probably won't worry that they don't recognize me either," Avery mused.

Phoebe studied the map. "Okay, I have another idea about how to make this work. I've noticed that the sidewalk right here"—Phoebe pointed to a spot on Spruce, right between the day care and Mocha Bean—"hasn't been cleared off very well lately. It's for sale, and the owner must not come and shovel after every storm. So Julie is going to be thinking about walking carefully and not falling— she'll be looking at her feet. She might not even notice if someone stealth"—Phoebe nodded at Avery—"just happens to join their group."

"Brilliant," Evan said, grinning at Phoebe.

"And if the others do say something, I can always create a distraction," Avery said thoughtfully. Clearly she was destined for CIA training.

"Good thinking," Phoebe said.

"It's a great plan," Evan said happily.

"It just might work," Avery agreed. Then she put her hands down on the table. "So now will you finally tell us the mysterious thing I'm going to give Julie at the critical moment in her sale?"

End of Day Sales Tally: Granville 183, Deerfield 188

CHAPTER 12

WEDNESDAY, DAY 10

Julie hefted the five boxes of Fantastic Five chocolate bars she was carrying from one arm to the other. She was walking down Spruce Street to Dandelion Day Care with two fifth graders who she didn't know that well. They'd volunteered to help out, and she was glad to have some extra arms. Julie had been thrilled when the director of the school, Ms. Fahadi, called to place a huge order for her staff holiday party. She'd requested that the boxes of chocolate be delivered this afternoon. Julie had made sure to confirm *this* order with Mr. Ryan so she did not have to worry that it might be another stupid prank.

Yes, Julie had been on board with the prank they'd

pulled on Granville Monday afternoon—what choice did she have after hearing Amber say Julie was too scared to give payback? Of course Julie had to respond by not only agreeing to Gabe's idea but volunteering to be the one to make the call. Otherwise she'd never shed the goody-goody label. But hopefully the successful prank on Monday, followed by a solid sale today, would give Deerfield the lead and earn Julie a new label: winner.

"Careful, there's some ice there," one of the fifth graders said, slipping slightly.

It snapped Julie out of her thoughts. The sidewalk here had been badly shoveled, and melting snow had refrozen, coating the uneven ground with ice. She rested her palm on a tree trunk as she stepped carefully over the slippery surface.

"Here, let me take some of your boxes," one of the fifth graders said. Julie glanced behind her. There were three girls there, not two—one of their friends must have joined the group at the last minute.

"Are you—" the first girl began, but just then the girl with long black hair skidded wildly on the ice and shrieked.

"Careful!" the third girl said, grabbing her arm. "It's like a skating rink out here." Together the three of them navigated to the other side of the ice while Julie followed slowly, focusing on putting one foot in front of the other. She did not want to drop her boxes—it would be bad for business if any of the precious chocolate inside broke.

"Okay, here we are," she said a moment later as the four of them arrived at the path leading up to Dandelion. The jungle gym and swing set were covered in snow, but this wide path had been well cleared for the toddlers who spent their days inside, and they were able to walk up without mishap.

"Hello, hello," Ms. Fahadi said, opening the door and ushering them in. "Come warm up! I'm so grateful you braved the cold for us." Dandelion's spacious lobby had benches and sets of colorful cubbies and was decorated with toddler art, which Julie saw was mostly swirls of scribbles. It was bright and welcoming even though Julie nearly tripped over a stray boot that had somehow fallen out of its owner's cubby.

"It was our pleasure," Julie said truthfully.

A group of little kids carrying musical instruments suddenly ran into the entryway. A few tried to blow on their recorders and bang their drums, but others had clearly decided the recorders were more fun for sword fighting and the drums were great to thump on the floor.

"The three-year-olds wanted to do a parade for you," Ms. Fahadi said with a laugh. "I hope you don't mind."

"No, they're totally cute," Julie said. They *were* pretty cute. Loud but cute.

Julie heard the phone ring. "I'll be right back," Ms. Fahadi said, walking into what Julie assumed was her office.

"Try blowing with just a little less force," a teacher told a little boy who was blowing on his recorder with all his might. It was a relief when he stopped.

"Hey," one of the fifth graders whispered, pulling lightly on Julie's free arm, the one that wasn't holding her boxes of bars.

Julie turned.

"Sorry to tell you this, but your breath kind of smells bad," the girl said, wincing slightly.

Oh no. Julie pressed her lips together to keep from breathing on anyone. This was so embarrassing. She swore she'd never breathe through her mouth again. But how could she be a good chocolate salesperson if she couldn't open her mouth to talk or smile—

"Want some gum?" the girl asked, passing Julie a stick.

"Thanks so much," Julie said gratefully, unwrapping it with her free hand. The gum was bright blue and felt a little stale in her mouth—she had to crunch down a bit before it softened up. But at least now she wouldn't breathe lunch fumes on Ms. Fahadi when she returned.

"Here we go," Ms. Fahadi said, sweeping out of her office.

But just then two of the parading kids started laughing rather maniacally, and a third began jumping up and down wildly. All three of them were looking at Julie.

"That is not funny," Ms. Fahadi said in a voice that was colder than the winter day outside as more kids fell into hysterics. "Children are very easily worked up by such pranks and very difficult to calm back down. And it's almost nap time."

"Julie, maybe we should—" one of the fifth graders started, but then a toddler barreled into her and she was too busy staying upright to finish.

Julie could not figure out what was going on. Her mouth felt oddly frothy—was there something wrong with the gum? And these kids did not seem ready to nap—they seemed more ready to riot.

"I'll thank you to leave now," Ms. Fahadi said as more children started going nuts, yelling, laughing, and running around the lobby while the teachers chased after them.

"You're so funny!" one of them shrieked at Julie, so loudly Julie worried her ears had been damaged.

Who knew toddlers could create such pandemonium?

Julie could not understand what had gone wrong. "But what about the chocolate?" she asked weakly. Her voice was furry from the froth—this gum was seriously off and Julie couldn't wait to spit it out.

"We won't be taking any chocolate today," Ms. Fahadi said, holding open the door. "And when we do get our chocolate, it will not be from you."

Julie and the others stumbled out into the cold as Ms. Fahadi shut the door firmly behind them. Julie could still hear the shrill laughter of the children through the thick door.

"What just happened?" Julie asked the two fifth graders who were standing next to her. She assumed they'd be as confused as she was, but instead they exchanged a glance.

"It's your . . . I don't think they liked . . ." one of them sputtered.

"What are you talking about?" Julie asked impatiently, but a cold dread was slinking down her back as she looked for the third girl with the long hair, the one who had given her the gum. But that girl was nowhere to be seen.

The fifth grader fumbled in her bag for a moment and then pulled out a small mirror that she handed to Julie. Julie took it, both wanting and not wanting to see herself. When she raised the mirror up in her free hand and gazed at her reflection, she gasped. It was worse than she had suspected: Her mouth frothed with blue bubbles that dripped down her chin. She looked like a clown that had just lost a food fight. No wonder the kids had gone hysterical and Ms. Fahadi had been so upset with her. Julie was a complete joke—and a bad one at that.

"What happened?" the other girl asked, puzzled.

"Granville," Julie said, anger bubbling lavalike in her stomach. "Granville and Evan Black are what happened!"

CHAPTER 13

WEDNESDAY, DAY 10

"Well, I guess I'll order a box," the clerk at the Imagination Emporium said.

Evan tried not to sigh. He and Phoebe had just taken nearly ten minutes to carefully and dramatically explain the Challenge to Mr. Waters, the man working at the toy and magic store, and they had hoped for a bigger pay-off. Especially since Evan had often bought pranking supplies—including the trick gum he hoped Julie was chewing right now—here over the years.

"The Fantastic Five bars are really incredible," Phoebe told him. "I bet you'll want more than that."

Mr. Waters, who wore a big purple bow tie and gold crown, pursed his lips. "I don't really like candy," he said, an attitude that did not fit with his silly costume or the colorful toys stuffed in every aisle of the store. "But they do sound good. Did you bring any single bars? I'd like to try one."

Evan shook his head regretfully.

"We ran out of single bars because they're so popular," Phoebe put in.

Evan was impressed with this lie—Phoebe was a truly good saleswoman.

"Well, why don't you bring some by tomorrow?" Mr. Waters said, just as the bell on the door of the store rang out.

"Okay, and should we put you down for one box now?" Evan asked. One was better than none.

But the customer who had walked in was now coming up to the counter with a small girl brandishing a foam sword. "Can you help us locate the section for dangerous knights?" he asked.

"Right away," Mr. Waters said to the customer as he straightened his crown. "Come back tomorrow," he told Evan and Phoebe.

"Will do," Phoebe said cheerfully, but Evan saw that her shoulders were slumping as she headed out of the store.

Evan followed, though he had to stop when the little girl whacked him on the leg with her sword. Nothing good was happening in this store this afternoon!

"That was a fail," Phoebe said glumly once they were both outside. The wind was whistling down Hazel Avenue, and Evan was quick to grab his hat out of his pocket to protect his ears from the bits of snow the breeze was whipping up.

"Yeah," Evan agreed. "But that was a good idea about selling single bars. I think Deerfield's been doing that— Ling Ling told me she saw Julie and Gabe carrying open boxes when they went to the post office."

"Then we should do it too," Phoebe said, perking up a bit. "It's a smart business move."

"It seems like it would definitely lead to more sales," Evan agreed as they turned onto Blossom.

"Or one sale," Phoebe said, wrinkling her nose. "I can't believe we haven't sold any boxes yet today." She fished around in her pocket and pulled out a mushed Sweet and Simple bar. "I bought this yesterday and it's kind of messed up, so I couldn't give it to Mr. Waters, but you want to split it?"

"Yeah, thanks," Evan said, his mouth watering as Phoebe pulled off the foil wrapper and split the thick, pure milk chocolate bar and handed Evan his half.

Evan popped the whole thing in his mouth, then closed his eyes as the creamy, rich chocolate melted on his tongue.

"How do they make these so good?" Phoebe asked a moment later, licking the last bit of her bar off her lips.

Evan shook his head. "I don't know, but whoever came up with the recipes for the Fantastic Five is a true genius."

Phoebe grinned. "Totally."

Evan was energized by the delicious snack. "Should we try the Shoe Horn?" he suggested. The small store, which had a huge blue horn in the window, had several employees and was just a few blocks away. Evan remembered from the spreadsheet that no one had been there yet.

"Okay," Phoebe said.

"Hey, it's the captains who are going to get the win for Granville!"

Evan turned and was delighted to see a group of sixth graders headed toward them.

"That's us," he said happily as one of the boys reached out to high-five him.

"Evan, what's up?" Rashid Alexander asked. He was in Evan's social studies class and had never greeted him before the Challenge.

"Granville rules!" another boy shouted as they headed on their way.

Yes, the contest was definitely getting Evan noticed!

"Do you think Avery managed to give Julie the gum yet?" Phoebe asked as they headed to the Shoe Horn.

"I hope so," Evan said, gleeful at the thought.

"You know, that reminds me," Phoebe said, turning to Evan, who nearly bumped into her. "You never told me what Julie did that made you so angry."

Evan's insides tensed up. "I'd rather not talk about it," he said shortly.

"Come on," Phoebe pleaded. "You have to tell me."

Evan did not care for this new, nosy side of Phoebe. "It's really no big thing," he told her.

"I can tell it is, though," Phoebe said. "And I'll keep it a secret, I promise. You can trust me."

But Evan shook his head firmly. Yes, he liked Phoebe, and he trusted her too. But there was no way he would ever tell her or anyone else what Julie had done to him that past summer at camp.

Phoebe's phone pinged, and she pulled it out, read her text, and then grinned at Evan. "It's from Avery," she said. "Julie fell for it. Deerfield lost the sale!"

And Julie had been—deservedly—humiliated in the process. Maybe Evan and Phoebe hadn't made their own sale today, but causing Deerfield to lose out on theirs? That was a real victory!

CHAPTER 14

WEDNESDAY, DAY 10

"I know she gets good grades," Amber was saying to Gabe, who was already over the conversation, and Jamal Johnson, a fifth grader who had also had the bad luck of showing up in sales headquarters in time to hear Amber rant. "And she made a big show of helping out with the prank on Monday. But we have to be realistic—Julie isn't the right co-captain for the Challenge."

Gabe had just come back to school after a disappointingly small sale at the clothing shop on Laurel Way and was not in the mood to hear Amber go on and on about Julie. Sure, Julie had been a bit reluctant to step up to the plate and prank Granville. But she'd done it and knocked it out of the park—what more did Amber want from her?

"Julie's just a goody-goody and—" Amber stopped short and gasped.

Gabe turned toward the door of the classroom and then gasped himself because charging into the room, her eyes blazing, was Julie.

"You are not going to believe what just happened," Julie began, as Jamal made a choking sound and Amber actually cried out.

"This," Julie said, pointing at her mouth, as though anyone in the room hadn't already noticed the navy bubbles oozing out. Gabe didn't know whether to be grossed out or very worried. "This is what Granville did to me when I was making a sale at Dandelion Day Care—a day care! I frothed like a wild animal in front of children," Julie raged as she began pacing around the room. "They went berserk because they thought I was some kind of misguided clown show, and we got thrown out with no sale, obviously."

Gabe's back stiffened. Humiliating Julie was bad, but a ruined sale too? This was a low blow by Granville.

"Granville is going down," Julie said, spitting out the words along with some more blue bubbles. "It's time for some serious payback."

Gabe couldn't help grinning as he glanced at Amber. She was blinking rapidly in response to this new Julie, who was about as far from a goody-goody as anyone could be. After a moment, Amber pulled on her backpack and slipped out.

"I'll go clean up, and then we're figuring out the most awful, humiliating, disgusting prank we can," Julie said, stalking out of the room.

"Wow," Jamal said, turning to Gabe. Jamal had been on Gabe's baseball team last spring, and he liked to win almost as much as Gabe did. "I've never seen Julie like that."

"Me neither," Gabe agreed. "I like it."

Jamal laughed, but then he turned serious. "Can I stay and help you guys? I want Deerfield to win the contest this year."

Jamal really was a pretty great guy.

Julie stormed back in. Her face was now much cleaner, though the edges of her mouth were still navy. "Before we figure out our next prank, I need some chocolate," she said.

Now she was talking!

Julie went and selected a Triple Crown and a S'more bar, then looked at Jamal. "What do you want?" she asked. "And it's on me—I got my allowance yesterday."

"A Triple Crown, definitely!" Jamal said. Julie took it from the box and put six dollars in the sales sheet collection carton to give to the office on their way out. Then she closed the door of the classroom, sat at the desk across from Gabe, and passed out the Fantastic Five bars.

"Okay, so do you guys have any great ideas?" she asked.

Gabe pulled open the foil wrapper of his S'more bar and nearly swooned at the intoxicating scent of milk chocolate, graham cracker, and marshmallow. But unfortunately even the magic of his chocolate bar did not inspire any prank ideas. And next to him Jamal was shaking his head.

"I don't either," Julie said. "I'm so mad I can't even think straight. But I did realize something when I was walking back from the day care drooling blue bubbles."

It was really hard not to laugh at that, and Gabe noticed Jamal's lips twist up as he made a small, strangled noise. Gabe probably had the same look on his face because Julie paused to eye them.

"This gum prank has Evan Black written all over it," she continued after they had been silenced. "Evan's a prank king, and I don't think we can come up with better pranks than he can."

Gabe scowled—how was this defeatist attitude helpful?

"So that means we should just steal his ideas," Julie said with a crafty smile. "He spent years pulling off jokes here at Deerfield, right? We all remember being pranked by him at some point. Gabe, you told me about the time he stuffed hundreds of balloons in the supply closet in English and you got to spend half the class chasing them down instead of taking a quiz. And I remember once last year he rigged a soda explosion in the middle of our science lab. So I say we pick the best ones and use them against him."

Gabe couldn't help being impressed—Julie had a whole criminal mastermind side to her!

"That must have been awesome," Jamal said. "I wish my class had a prank king—less work, more jokes."

"Yeah, it's funny until it happens to you," Julie said sourly, and Jamal winced.

"Sorry," he said.

"It's okay because we're going to get him back," Julie said firmly. "There was also that time he put plastic bugs in Ms. Teixeira's desk."

"That was really funny," Gabe said, remembering how Ms. Teixeira had screamed but then laughed along with the rest of the class for about five minutes straight.

And then Gabe remembered something else that had happened in Ms. Teixeira's class. "Hey, I know what we should do," he exclaimed. "Itching powder!"

Julie was so delighted by this, she clapped her hands. "Yes! Jamal, last year Evan sprinkled itching powder on Ian on April Fools'."

"That was hysterical," Gabe said, grinning at the memory of Ian scratching like a madman. Picturing Evan suffering the same fate made Gabe feel as good as though he'd just hit a home run out of the park.

"Okay, so that's what we'll do—sprinkle itching powder on Evan and Phoebe," Julie said. "Where do we get it?"

"Let me find out," Jamal said, getting up and going over to a computer.

As Jamal typed, Gabe bit into his S'more bar and was momentarily distracted by the smooth chocolate, the crispy graham cracker chunks, molassesy and sweet, the cloud of sugary marshmallow. The S'more bar was true perfection.

"Imagination Emporium has slow-acting itching powder in their joke section," Jamal announced a moment later. "It takes a few hours to activate after you put it on, but that should be okay. And I can pick it up this afternoon."

"Perfect," Julie said. "Thanks."

"So now we just have to figure out how to get the powder on the co-captains of Granville," Gabe started.

"Especially Evan," Julie said quickly.

"Especially Evan," Gabe agreed. "And it has to be in the morning, so that by the afternoon they're way too itchy to do anything but go home."

"They might even break out in hives," Jamal said, biting into his Triple Crown.

"Even better," Julie muttered, and Gabe stifled a laugh.

"So how do we do it?" Jamal asked, clearly considering himself part of things now.

"Maybe we could hide behind the door of the school and jump out and douse them with it," Gabe suggested, popping the last bite of S'more bar into his mouth.

Julie looked worried. "That would make a scene and get us in trouble."

"Well, maybe we could wait for them before they actually walk onto school grounds and dump it on them Gatorade-style," Gabe said. That would really be fun.

But Julie was shaking her head. "We can't throw a jar of itching powder all over them like they just won the Super Bowl," she said. "Then they'd know we contaminated them with something and go home and take a shower."

Julie might not be a goody-goody right now, but she was certainly being a downer. "Do you have a better idea?" Gabe asked, crumpling up his S'more bar wrapper and wishing he had money for a second one.

"As a matter of fact, yes," Julie said somewhat smugly. "And, Jamal, we're going to need your help to pull it off."

Jamal had some chocolate on the side of his mouth as he smiled. "I'm in," he said. "What do you need me to do?"

"What I'm thinking," Julie began, leaning forward, "is that Gabe and I find Phoebe and Evan on the sidewalk in front of Granville tomorrow morning and get into an argument with them."

"That'll be easy," Gabe said, and Jamal laughed.

"Then, Jamal, while they're distracted, you can come up behind them and sprinkle some of the powder onto them," Julie finished. "But subtly, so they don't feel it."

Jamal pressed his fingertips together. "They'll be wearing coats and stuff, so I'm not sure it'll get on them."

That was a good point.

"No, not right away," Julie said. Gabe could see she was already ten steps ahead of both him and Jamal, and once again he was impressed with this pranking-mastermind side of Julie. "But when they get inside and take off their coats and scarves and stuff, some of the powder is bound to shake off on them."

Now Jamal was nodding. "The website said this stuff is potent, so it shouldn't take much," he agreed.

"Exactly," Julie said with a smile.

"Sounds like we have a plan," Gabe said happily. He was kind of hoping that devising such an awesome prank would inspire Julie to treat them all to a second Fantastic Five bar.

But Julie had stood up and was gathering her things. "Just remember, get the powder on Evan first," she said. "We want it on Phoebe too, but he's the number one priority."

"Got it," Jamal said. "See you guys tomorrow."

"When we outprank the prank king," Gabe said, and both Jamal and Julie high-fived him at that.

End of Day Sales Tally: Granville 196, Deerfield 192

CHAPTER 15

THURSDAY, DAY II

The sky was gray as Phoebe headed to school on Thursday morning, but her thoughts were sunny—and that was due to numbers: sales numbers. As of yesterday afternoon's new numbers, Granville had pulled ahead again! Phoebe had finally evened the playing field so that their school could actually compete. Plus, their epic prank on Deerfield had gone off without a hitch. Word of Julie frothing blue bubbles had spread through the student body of Granville, and Phoebe and Evan had both received numerous congratulatory texts yesterday afternoon and evening. And today, to fully bask in this glory, Evan had suggested they meet at the oak tree by the sidewalk in front of school so that they could go in together for a victory march.

When Phoebe turned at the corner of Chestnut and Walnut, she spotted Evan already under the tree. As she hurried to meet him, she saw a group of students stop when they came to Evan. Phoebe couldn't help smiling—no doubt it was more people congratulating him on yesterday's winning move. She picked up her pace even more so that she was now nearly jogging—she wanted to be part of the celebration too. It would be fun to talk over all the details of how they executed their prank.

But as she got close, she saw that two of the people who had stopped were none other than their archnemeses, Julie and Gabe. And two against one was not an equation she cared for.

"You have a lot of nerve showing up at our school," Phoebe said, marching into the middle of the group, her fists clenched.

"I just wanted to say thanks for the gum," Julie said with a biting tone Phoebe would have admired from anyone else. "It was very refreshing."

"Glad it didn't make you blue," Evan said with a huge grin.

Phoebe cackled—score one for Granville in the fabulous pun department!

Julie, on the other hand, just wrinkled her nose while

Gabe scowled. Clearly no one at Deerfield had a good sense of humor.

"And I hope it didn't hurt your sale," Phoebe said, unable to keep from sounding gleeful.

Julie's eyes narrowed. "Oh, no, the frothing blue bubbles made me the hit of the day care," she said with heavy sarcasm that only increased Phoebe's glee. "They asked me to come back and read the kids a nap-time story today because they appreciated that so much."

"I guess next time you'll listen to your mom," Evan said sweetly.

Julie and Gabe glanced at each other, confused.

"Never take candy—or, in this case, gum—from a stranger," Evan crowed.

Phoebe chuckled. Evan was really funny when he wanted to be!

"Thanks for the advice," Julie said, rolling her eyes.

Just then someone pulled at Phoebe's turquoise-and-plum scarf. Phoebe jerked away, then turned to see who had been such a klutz. A tall boy with a fuzzy black Steelers hat was looking at her sheepishly. "Watch it," Phoebe told him.

"Sorry," he said.

Phoebe reached up and readjusted her scarf, then turned back to Julie and Gabe.

"So what brings you to the school that's going to win the Chocolate Challenge this year?" she asked.

Gabe grinned in a way that Phoebe did not care for. "Oh, nothing special," he said.

"We were just in the neighborhood," Julie said, biting back a smile.

Phoebe and Evan exchanged a look. Were Gabe and Julie trying to introduce some new factor to the equation?

"You can move along now," Phoebe said, deciding not to give them a chance to add anything.

"The quicker the better," Evan added.

Phoebe suddenly noticed that the same boy who had pulled on her scarf was now standing right behind Evan. "Hey," she said, just as the boy bumped into Evan, who pitched forward.

"Sorry, sorry," the guy said, backing away quickly. He disappeared into the crowd heading toward Granville.

"I guess we'll be going, then," Gabe said. He and Julie headed rather abruptly down the sidewalk.

"And don't come back," Evan called after them. Then he looked at Phoebe, puzzled. "What was that about?"

Phoebe shook her head as she watched their nemesis co-captains turn at the corner and head toward Deerfield. "I have no idea," she replied.

* * *

Phoebe spent the day accepting congratulations from her classmates and keeping an eye out for some kind of retaliation from Deerfield. But there was no sign that anything was amiss, and by the end of the day, Phoebe had nearly forgotten the unsettling early-morning visit. In fact, for the first time in weeks she had something other than the sale on her mind: Over the course of the day, it had become obvious that Phoebe had gotten lice.

Sitting in her last-period class, Phoebe was sure of it. There had been an outbreak in her third-grade class, and nearly every student had been afflicted. At first, Phoebe had secretly *wanted* lice. She thought it might be exciting to miss a day of school. That was before she was attacked by the insidious insects that made her short black curls a personal torture chamber. Her head had itched to distraction, and missing school had been small consolation for her suffering.

Now she was getting flashbacks to that awful time. The itching was driving her crazy. She didn't want to attract the attention of her history teacher, so she tried to subtly scratch her scalp with a pencil as she waited for the day to end, but her skin was so inflamed that scratching barely helped. She was worried that a long night of lice shampoo, laundry, and a lice comb awaited her. It was not helping that the heat at school seemed to be up unnaturally high and that the halls were baking with the smell of that day's unappetizing lunch entrée of meat loaf.

When the bell rang, she pulled her winter hat over her hair and ran toward sales headquarters. There was no way she was skipping her chocolate sales work, but maybe the hat would contain the lice. Yuck.

As she entered the classroom, she saw Evan was looking at the sales sheet to direct a group of sixth graders on where to sell. The group was oddly silent—hopefully that meant they were feeling very serious about their sale, though it was a bit strange.

"Hey, Evan, I'm here!" she called.

Evan looked up to greet her, and Phoebe did her best not to recoil at the sight of him. No wonder the group had been silent—they were clearly horrified by the raging red splotches covering Evan's face and neck!

Phoebe rubbed her palms against her hat and tried to figure out how to tell Evan he had been transformed into a ghoul.

"Hi," he said, walking over to her. "Are you okay?"

Why was he asking her this when he had clearly just broken out with the plague?

"Yeah, I'm great," Phoebe said, scratching at her neck—were the lice now migrating across her body to spread their evil itching even more? "What about you? Are you feeling okay?"

Evan swiped at one of the spots on his cheek while frowning at her. "Yeah, I'm fine," he said. "Though I'm kind of hot. I think the heat got turned up too high. It's making me kind of itchy."

"Yeah, me too," Phoebe said. Was it the heat in the building that was making her head crawl? That would definitely be better than lice.

"Um, guys, the heat is normal," Avery said, coming up to them looking concerned.

"No, it got turned up too high," Phoebe said firmly. She had already taken off her sweater and wished she had worn a T-shirt instead of a thick long-sleeved shirt beneath it.

Ms. Chase walked in. "Hi guys, I just—whoa," she said, stopping midstride as she caught sight of Evan. "Okay, why are you both here and not in the nurse's office?" she asked.

Phoebe glanced at Evan because she was kind of wondering the same thing. Though why had Ms. Chase included her in the question? Unless—

"Do I have awful red spots all over me like you?" Phoebe asked Evan.

"Wait, I have those spots too?" Evan asked. "Because you are covered."

"It looks like you both have some kind of rash," Ms. Chase said, ushering them toward the door. "Stop by the nurse or, better yet, just go on home."

"But what about the sale?" Phoebe asked, horrified at the thought of missing a whole afternoon of sales time.

"No sales for either of you today," Ms. Chase said firmly. "Go home and get some cream for those rashes. I don't want to see either of you back here until you are fully recovered." And with that she shut the door.

"I can't believe we both got a rash," Phoebe said, turning to Evan. Then she took a step back because Evan's face had turned even redder than the red spots, his hands were clenched, and his body was shaking.

"This is no rash," he hissed.

Had the spots gone to his brain?

"It's—" Phoebe began, but Evan interrupted.

"Itching powder," he finished.

Phoebe shook her head because that made no sense. Then she scratched at her cheek, which was heating up with itchiness.

"*Julie*," Evan said. "And Gabe." He glared at Phoebe as though she was supposed to get it. "When they came by before school, they weren't just strolling by. They were here to cover us with itching powder."

"But they were here this morning and I didn't start itching until after lunch," Phoebe said, concerned Evan was getting paranoid. Yes, Julie and Gabe were sneaky, but it was a stretch to think they could have pulled this off.

"They used slow-acting itching powder," Evan said, scratching fiercely at his neck. "It's the best kind because it doesn't go into effect for a few hours. And it doesn't just make you itch—it makes you hot too."

Phoebe did feel like she'd tumbled into an oven. But she still wasn't convinced. "Neither of them touched us, though, and—oh," she finished, sucking in the word as she remembered the clumsy boy who pulled her scarf and bumped into Evan. "They had a secret agent!" Phoebe was shouting. Two little kids walking by looked nervous and hurried past. But Phoebe was too busy being outraged to care that she looked slightly deranged. "That guy who bumped into you—it wasn't a coincidence—he was putting the powder on us!"

"Yeah," Evan said, scrubbing his head with his knuckles. "You're right; that's how they did it. I can't believe we weren't more suspicious when they showed up here."

"That's a mistake we won't make again," Phoebe said,

now rubbing at her back, which was starting to heat up. The powder was alarmingly effective!

"Tell me about it," Evan muttered as they started toward the door of the school. Phoebe was looking forward to being outside in the frigid cold—in fact she was considering rolling around in the snow to see if it would cool her off.

"This stuff is torturous," she told Evan, who nodded. His spots had gotten even redder.

"We have to get home and take baths," he said. "With baking soda. And you might need hydrocortisone cream after that too."

At this point Phoebe was wishing she could climb out of her skin it was so uncomfortable. They were outside now, but even the ice-tinged wind was not helping.

Phoebe clawed at her neck and then began to run. Evan, who was rubbing his head, was right behind her.

"After you get home," Evan said, panting slightly as they got to the corner and he turned left toward his house, "call me. Because we are going to get them for this."

"That's a promise!" Phoebe called as she raced for home.

CHAPTER 16

THURSDAY, DAY 11

"Wait, is that them?" Julie asked, peeking from behind the tree where she, Gabe, and Jamal were hiding outside Granville. She squinted at the two figures coming down the steps of the school.

"I think it is," Gabe said, leaning forward.

"It definitely is," Jamal confirmed. "That's Phoebe's scarf—I remember it from this morning."

Julie was holding her breath as the three of them stood still and waited for a sign that their biggest prank yet had worked.

"She's scratching her neck!" Gabe crowed in triumph.

"And he looks like he's going to rub his scalp off," Jamal said.

The three of them began laughing as their nemeses took off running.

"Score one for Deerfield," Julie said, utterly delighted by their success. Seeing Evan and Phoebe racing home with itchy skin instead of going out to sell chocolate almost made up for what she had been through with the gum. Almost.

"I'd say we score two for that," Gabe said happily as they started back toward town. "Because we took out both co-captains at once."

Julie nodded—it was an excellent point.

"The best part is that we used Evan's own trick against him," Jamal added, his boots scuffing in the snow piled up along the sidewalk. "Which was a great idea," he told Julie, who could not help being pleased at the compliment.

"Welcome to the dark side," Gabe said in a Darth Vader voice.

No one was going to be calling Julie a goody-goody once word got out about this prank! She grinned at Gabe. "Thanks," she said. "It's good to be here."

"Hey, that was awesome how you guys got Granville," Max Sherman called to Julie on Friday afternoon. He was with a group of boys who would normally walk right past her without a glance. But ever since word of the itching-powder incident got around, Julie had transformed into someone people stopped to compliment in the halls, even though the final bell had just rung and boys like Max had places to go. And that gave Julie a delicious fizziness that had made the whole day sweet.

"You had them running home like crybabies!" Jake Shiro said. "Nice."

"Thanks," Julie said. She noticed Amber passing, a frown on her face, and that made Julie smile even more. Not such a goody-goody now, was she, not with a crowd gathering to tell her how she had totally taken the Granville co-captains down!

"We're going to outsell them, right?" Max asked.

For a brief second, Julie wasn't sure what he meant, but then of course she remembered the chocolate-selling part of the contest. "Absolutely," she said. Then she headed for sales headquarters, feeling terrific.

Gabe was already there when Julie arrived, looking down at the sales sheet in his hand.

"Hey," Julie said cheerily, ready to talk more about their big victory against Granville.

Gabe looked up, and Julie saw that the corners of his mouth were turning down slightly. "Did you know that we've fallen behind on sales?" he asked.

"No, I guess I didn't notice," Julie said. Had they? She

didn't really want to notice. She wanted to focus on their next big prank. "I guess we've been spending a lot of time winning the prank war against Granville."

"Yeah, that's been great," Gabe agreed, finally smiling. But then he looked down at the sheet again. "We should probably get some big sales today, though."

Just then Julie heard a muffled cry in the hall. "What was that?" she asked Gabe, who frowned and shook his head.

"I don't know," he said.

Julie walked over to the door and peered out, but the hall was nearly empty. The janitor was opening up a closet at one end, and at the other, a few bundled-up students were heading toward the front door. No one looked like they'd heard anything out of the ordinary.

"It was nothing," she reported to Gabe as she came back in.

"Okay, well, like I was saying, we need to sell some boxes today. Get our numbers back up," Gabe said.

"Sure," Julie said, still not wanting to think about it. "But maybe we can have some of the other kids handle the sales. I had a great idea for another prank."

Gabe gave her a long look, kind of like he had never seen her before.

"What?" Julie asked. Did she have something on her face?

"Nothing," Gabe said, shaking his head. "It's just—I thought you'd be more worried about our sales numbers."

Julie shrugged and tried to keep up the appearance of being nonchalant. Goody-goodies worried about sales numbers, not rock-star pranksters who got stopped in the halls by boys like Max Sherman and Jake Shiro. And that's who Julie was now: a rock-star prankster who did what it took to win both the prank war and the Challenge. Not some goody-goody who stressed about numbers all day.

End of Day Sales Tally: Granville 215, Deerfield 220

CHAPTER 17

FRIDAY, DAY 12

"You look like you got attacked by giant mosquitoes," a girl informed Evan as he stood in front of his locker after the final bell.

Evan tried to smile, like he found her remark amusing, but it was hard. Despite two baking soda baths and a tube of hydrocortisone, he still *felt* like he'd been attacked by giant mosquitoes, and after a day of hearing about yesterday's epic itching powder disaster, he was tired of being laughed at. Making jokes was fun; being the butt of them was not. And that was what he was, the butt of the joke. Yes, Evan had entered this contest determined to earn a title for himself—but Evan "Laughingstock" Black was not what he'd had in mind.

Of course there was only one way to remedy it: pull a prank more epic than itching powder on Deerfield. It was a tall order, but to regain his proper title of Evan "Prank King" Black, it had to be done—and Evan was pretty sure he'd come up with the prank that would seal the deal.

Evan closed his locker, pulled his backpack over his shoulder, and started down the hall to Granville sales headquarters.

"Wow, it's like you caught mutant chicken pox," a boy passing said, and all his friends laughed.

Evan gritted his teeth and did his best to laugh too—after all, the worst thing he could do was turn into Evan "Bad Sport" Black. But the fake laugh scraped at his throat.

Phoebe was already at headquarters looking over their sales sheet. Her brown skin had the same red tint of irritation as Evan's, and her red spots were the same scabby bumps. They really did look like they'd caught mutant chicken pox.

"Hi," Evan said, going up to Phoebe. She looked at him and shook her head.

"It's been a long day," she said with a sigh.

"Tell me about it," Evan agreed. "If one more person has something to say about my spots . . ."

"Yup," Phoebe agreed before he finished the thought. Not that he needed to—he knew she got it.

A few volunteers came in for Fantastic Five boxes and sale assignments, but once the room had cleared, Phoebe closed the door and leaned back against it. "Okay, Wizard of Pranks, what's our next move?" she asked.

Evan made a metal note that the name "Wizard of Pranks" had a real ring to it and then sat on the desk to share his plan. "Remember how we got really hot because of the itching powder yesterday?"

Phoebe's nose scrunched. "All too well," she said.

Evan snickered. "Yeah, it was bad, but it gave me an excellent idea: I think we should turn up the thermostat at Deerfield so that all their Fantastic Five bars melt!"

Phoebe's face lit up. "Oh, wow," she said. "I love it. That's perfect—make it so that there's no way they can beat us in sales."

"And make it so Julie and Gabe look like awful co-captains because they allowed their supply of chocolate to be breached," Evan said. The thought of humiliating Gabe and especially Julie was even more satisfying than winning the Challenge.

"So how do we pull it off?" Phoebe asked. "Because getting to the Deerfield thermostat sounds complicated."

Evan grinned and pulled on his coat. "Remember, I used to go to Deerfield," he said. "And that means I know a few secrets about the school."

*　　*　　*

Students did not and, as far as Evan knew, had never used the side door of Deerfield Elementary. That was because it led out to the giant Dumpster that held the cafeteria remains. It smelled foul even in cold weather. Which made it the perfect entry point.

"Oh, man. What do they serve in the Deerfield cafeteria?" Phoebe asked, holding her nose as they slipped past the Dumpster. "That is foul!"

"The same gross stuff we get at Granville," Evan said absently. He was busy hoping that the Deerfield cafeteria trash schedule hadn't changed since last year. But sure enough, after only a moment, a cafeteria worker pushed open the heavy side door, a bag of trash slung over his shoulder.

"We forgot something in our lockers. Can we come in?" Evan asked quickly.

He was counting on the bad smell and cold air to be enough of a distraction that the worker would not ask questions. And sure enough he just waved them inside. Step one of the plan was complete! But the bigger challenges lay before them.

Once inside the school Evan was hit by a sudden wave of nostalgia. Deerfield smelled the same: a mix of lemon cleaner, wet wool, and sweaty socks. It was yucky but also homey in a way that Granville wasn't. After all, Evan had lost his first tooth in the Deerfield cafeteria and learned to read, add, and use a computer in these classrooms, and it was here that he first became Evan "Prank King" Black. But there was no time to be sentimental, so Evan pressed ahead.

"The thermostat is in the basement," Evan told Phoebe in a low voice as they both pulled their hoods up just a little higher. "This way."

"How do you know these things?" she asked quietly as they walked quickly toward the back stairs.

Evan couldn't help puffing out his chest just a bit. "When you make a practice of pulling off pranks, this is the stuff you need to know," he said. "There are three entry points to the basement, so it's a great way to travel around the school undetected." And it was on one of these undetected forays that Evan had taken note of the school thermostat.

Two students were coming down the hall, and Evan was dismayed to see he knew them. But luckily there was a water fountain nearby, so he rushed over and bent down, his back to his former classmates.

They passed without stopping. Crisis averted.

"We should hurry," he said to Phoebe, picking up his pace.

They were halfway down the basement stairs when one of the janitors called from behind. "Hey, kids, basement's off-limits." Evan recognized the voice as Mr. Peterson's.

"Okay, sorry," Evan said, sighing.

He and Phoebe headed back up the stairs.

"That was bad timing," Phoebe said. "But you know another way down, right?"

"Yeah, there are two other staircases, but one is close enough that I think Mr. Peterson might see us," Evan said. "And if he catches us down there, it'll be a problem."

"So let's just take the other staircase," Phoebe said as though it were obvious. Which it was except—

"That one goes right by Deerfield sales headquarters," Evan said.

"Oh," Phoebe said, her shoulders sagging. Being seen by Julie and Gabe would totally ruin their prank.

"But there's no other way to get to the thermostat. We'll have to try it," Evan said. "Keep your hood up and move fast." He led the way toward the hall that passed room 103.

It was hot with winter coats on, but the thought that soon it would be even hotter—chocolate-melting hotter—made the discomfort tolerable.

Evan sped up even more as they rounded the corner. Room 103 was on the right. Luckily the door was closed, but the light was on—clearly someone was inside, and Evan had a good bet on just who it was. Phoebe was next to him, and she ducked her head as they came up to the room. Evan did the same and turned his face to one side so that if Julie or Gabe happened to look out of the classroom just as they passed, all they'd see would be two figures in winter coats rushing by. A totally normal thing to see at the end of the day. But still, his heart was pounding as they passed room 101.

". . . should probably get some big sales today . . ." Evan heard Gabe say as they sped past 103. Evan couldn't help grinning an evil grin at that. Yes, they better get good sales today because by Monday their chocolate supply would be ruined!

Evan was about to breathe a sigh of relief, when Phoebe, who was still looking down, bumped into a water fountain and yelped. They both froze. And then Evan heard a classroom door opening behind them.

"Hurry," he whispered, his heart once again pounding. He and Phoebe nearly sprinted to the corner, and Evan heard the door close. But was someone coming after them? He couldn't risk turning around to check.

"The basement stairs are over here," he whispered, grabbing Phoebe's arm.

A moment later, they had run down the steps into the gloomy basement, and there, Evan finally breathed his sigh of relief.

"That was close," he said.

"Sorry I wasn't looking where I was going," Phoebe said, rubbing her hip where she'd bumped into the fountain. "I don't think I'm cut out to be a spy."

Evan agreed but decided not to say so. "The important thing is that we made it," he said, starting toward the far corner where the thermostat was. They passed boxes of supplies and a few broken desks and then reached their final destination.

"You should do the honors," Phoebe said, gesturing grandly toward the small metal box that would bring Deerfield's downfall.

Evan pushed the up button to the highest setting: ninety degrees. Hot enough to melt chocolate but not disturb any of the animals that lived in the science lab or younger classrooms. "Done," he said. "By Monday morning, Deerfield's chocolate will be a melted mess."

He and Phoebe high-fived and then headed to the back stairs. Mr. Peterson was long gone, so they slipped through

the cafeteria a second time and then out into the icy afternoon. Snow was starting to fall, and the flakes were
soothing on Evan's spots. But not as soothing as the thought
of the Deerfield co-captains discovering their ruined chocolate on Monday morning!

End of Day Sales Tally: Granville 222, Deerfield 229

CHAPTER 18

MONDAY, DAY 15

Gabe overslept on Monday morning and had to run the last two blocks to avoid being late for homeroom. But when he rounded the corner of Oak and Dogwood, nearly skidding on a small patch of black ice, a surprising sight met his eyes. What looked like the entire student body was standing in front of Deerfield. For a moment, Gabe worried that there was a fire or some other disaster that was preventing students from entering the building. But as he came closer, he saw that people were smiling. Big smiles, as though it was somehow everyone's birthday on the exact same day.

His friends Joe, Khai, and Erlan were standing at the end of the path, so Gabe made his way over to them. "What's going on?" he asked.

"The thermostat went nuts over the weekend," Joe said happily. "And now it's broken, so they think it might not be warm enough for us to have school today."

This was even better than a birthday! "For real?" Gabe asked, his thoughts going to all the wonderful things that could be done on an unexpected holiday.

"Video games at my house if we're off," Khai said. "My mom works from home, and she won't mind if we're there."

"I—" Gabe began, but just then Principal Martin appeared on the steps of the school and everyone quieted.

"As some of you have already learned, on Friday the school thermostat was accidentally set to the highest setting, which triggers an automatic shutdown," the principal said. "It will take several hours to reverse the situation and heat the school to an acceptable temperature, so school is canceled for today."

She was still speaking, but it was impossible to hear over the loud cheering that had overtaken the yard.

"Awesome!" Erlan yelled, high-fiving Khai.

Ainyr, a girl in Gabe's science class, ran by with her friend Amirah but paused when she saw Gabe. "Julie's looking for you," she reported, and then the two girls took off to enjoy their day.

Avi, Khai's younger brother, came up breathless. "I called Mom, and she said we can get snacks on the way home."

"Great," Khai said. "You coming, Gabe?"

But Gabe had to shake his head. A day of video games with his friends would be awesome, but he and Julie had to take advantage of this extra time to up their sales numbers. And with the whole day in front of them, they could sell a *lot* of boxes.

He made his way through the celebrating students to Julie, who was near the front steps of the school talking to Jamal and a few of the other regular volunteers. When she saw Gabe, she beckoned him over.

"This is great, right?" Gabe asked, his feet crunching down on the snowdrift next to them.

"And it gets even better," Julie said. Her eyes were glowing. "Because it turns out this was not some random mistake. I heard Mr. Peterson say that Friday two students were trying to get into the basement and he thinks they're the ones that set the thermostat on its highest setting. So it's thanks to them we have the day off."

She looked at Gabe like this was some fantastic news. But who cared how it had happened?

Gabe shrugged. "So?"

"So can't you guess who those two students were?" Julie asked in an unnaturally loud voice.

Gabe did not like how the conversation had turned into a quiz. "Why does it matter?" he asked.

"Because obviously one of them, who used to be a student here, thought it would be a great prank to turn up the heat and melt our chocolate," Julie explained.

Gabe didn't understand why she was carrying on about this, because so what if—and that's when he got it. "So Granville tried to prank us, but instead they gave us a free day off?" he asked, not believing this incredible turn of good luck. And bad pranking.

"Yup," Julie said, grinning.

Gabe was grinning too. Those fools at Granville had probably really sweat sneaking into Deerfield, crossing into enemy territory believing they were pulling off the best prank yet, only to have it completely backfire in their faces.

"Pretty sweet," Gabe said. "And now we have the whole day to—"

"Go to the joke section of the Imagination Emporium and plan our next prank," Julie interrupted. The other volunteers cheered at this, and Julie beamed.

"I was going to say we should sell a ton of boxes," Gabe told her. They had to get their sales numbers up if they wanted to actually WIN the contest—had Julie forgotten that?

"Sure, we can do that too," Julie said in a dismissive tone. But then she turned to the other volunteers who Gabe was starting to think of as her followers. "But first we need to plan how to take down Granville once and for all!"

Gabe was pushed to the side as people began offering up ideas, each more absurd and possibly illegal than the last. Gabe looked at Julie, who was not just glowing anymore—she was fevered in her frenzy to demolish their rivals. What had happened to his even-tempered co-captain who cared about rules and working hard to win the sales contest? He couldn't believe this was the same person who had needed a pretty hard push just to pull off one simple prank two weeks earlier.

Gabe had only been kidding when he welcomed Julie to the dark side, but now, as he watched her, he couldn't help thinking there really was a disturbance in the Force.

"Hey, what if we get a few of these and put them in their chocolate boxes?" Julie asked, pointing at a bin of grisly plastic severed heads.

Their group had arrived at the Imagination Emporium, much to the dismay of the store clerk who was keeping a careful eye on them from his perch behind the counter. Not that Gabe could blame the guy—Julie and the four followers who'd tagged along were acting pretty scary.

"That would be hysterical," one of the girls said, laughing loudly.

"Not really," Gabe said, alarmed by how realistic the heads were. "It could actually scare a customer and give them a stroke or something."

"Right," Julie said, backing away from the severed body parts display. But Gabe saw her roll her eyes and heard someone mutter, "Spoilsport."

Before Gabe could process the sheer absurdity of someone calling him—*him*, the most competitive person on the planet according to his baseball coach—a spoilsport, Julie was offering up another insane prank idea.

"Maybe we can rig all their sprinklers to go off at once," she was saying, making the followers laugh yet again.

Gabe didn't even recognize this Julie, who was so intent on destroying their rivals for the win that she had morphed into some kind of prank warlord. Of course Gabe wanted to win too, but not at the risk of getting thrown in prison. Julie had truly lost it, and the saddest part was that Gabe was the only one there to veto the insane things she was suggesting. Everyone but Gabe was acting like this was the battle of the zombie apocalypse, not just a small-town chocolate sale.

"Or we could—" Julie began, but Gabe had had enough.

"We should do a stink bomb," he said firmly, stopping in front of the display. It was time to get out of here and start selling chocolate—and a stink bomb was a perfectly respectable prank. "It says the bombs are silent and just one smells like a hundred rotten eggs."

"Let's get a hundred and put them in all their boxes," Julie said, nearly tripping over the store's magic wand rack in her enthusiasm over her latest terrible idea.

"No," Gabe said, a lone voice of reason over the approval of the followers. "Just a few are enough. And it's going to be hard to even manage that."

"One of us can bring in one of our boxes with some stink bombs inside and swap it out for one of theirs," Julie said. "They'll never notice."

It was the first good idea she'd had all day.

"But if we can do it with one, why not do it with ten or twenty?" she went on, ruining it.

"No, just one box," Gabe said.

"What a goody-goody," one of the followers muttered.

And Gabe suddenly realized that the kid was referring to him.

CHAPTER 19

MONDAY, DAY 15

When the final bell rang, all Phoebe wanted to do was head home, never to return again. The day had started out bad, with Phoebe and Evan trying to live down the itching-powder debacle and still sporting a few red scabs. But it had become a complete fiasco times a million when word began trickling in of their newest failure: the thermostat prank.

It started in second period, when the news of Deerfield's unexpected day off hit the school, followed quickly by the cause: the thermostat being turned up too high, which triggered its shutdown. At first, Phoebe had been certain she and Evan would never be linked to it—no one had seen them there after all. But what Phoebe had not counted on was Evan's pride. He had been so certain of their prank's success that apparently when he got to school this morning he had boasted about it to Avery. Avery had told a few of the other volunteers, and so by the start of third period, everyone in fifth and sixth grade knew just who had handed Deerfield their day off.

Thus had begun the most humiliating day of Phoebe's life.

"So I guess we're losing this prank war by about a thousand to zero," Roy Butler said bitterly to Phoebe as she walked down the hall.

"Well—" Phoebe began.

"And we're going to lose the Challenge too, right?" he interrupted, shaking his head like Phoebe had single-handedly ruined everything.

"I'm not . . ." Phoebe tried again, but Roy just walked away. Which was probably for the best because what could she say? Phoebe had wanted to make things fair. The contest favored Deerfield, and as co-captain, she thought it was her responsibility to change that, to make the Challenge a balanced equation. But her attempts to even things out had not lead to that balanced equation; they'd lead to chaos theory, an unpredictable branch of math that Phoebe had never enjoyed. It resulted in things like a messy prank war, which Granville was losing and losing badly. Phoebe, with Evan's help, was responsible for disgracing the sales team, the Challenge, her school, her town, and most of all herself.

It was hard to walk down the hall with this knowledge heavy on her shoulders. The angry looks of her classmates did not help. But although the one thing Phoebe wanted to do was flee Granville, contract a rare but not fatal illness, and be homeschooled until college, she couldn't leave—not yet. Not when Granville was completely vulnerable to attack.

When Phoebe finally arrived at sales headquarters, it was a small and sad group that waited inside. Saddest of all was Evan. A few spots had scabbed on his cheeks, making him look as though he'd spent the night in a Dumpster, but it was the stricken expression on his face that was the worst part. Evan prided himself on his pranking skills, but he had been completely and fully outpranked, which had to sting. In fact, sorry as she felt for herself, she felt even worse for Evan. But that didn't make her any less angry at him.

"I was thinking how we can prank them next," Evan said, hurrying over to Phoebe. "What if we get into their chocolate supply and cover it with hot pepper?"

"We'd probably start a craze of people loving hot pepper chocolate and then everyone in town would buy their bars and not ours," Phoebe snapped.

"I don't think—" Evan began, but Phoebe shook her head firmly.

"We have to really think through our next move," she told him. "But before we do that, we have to protect ourselves. Deerfield had the whole day off, and you know they weren't just playing video games. They were plotting their next move against us."

Evan's face went pale at this. "You're right," he said, sagging against a desk.

"And the first thing we need to do is protect our chocolate," Phoebe said. She had spent much of gym considering the most likely outcome of their failed prank, and since they had tried to go after Deerfield's chocolate, it seemed only logical that now Deerfield would come after theirs.

"Yeah, that makes sense," Evan agreed, standing back up.

Despite her irritation at Evan's bad prank plan, she couldn't help appreciate that at this point he knew her so well she didn't even have to spell things out.

"I was thinking we should put it all in there," Phoebe said, nodding toward the supply closet at the back of the room. "And then talk to Ms. Chase about getting a lock for it."

"Do you think she'll agree to that?" Avery asked. She was one of the few volunteers who had showed up, and Phoebe was glad she was there—they'd need help moving the Fantastic Five—they still had an awful lot of boxes.

"We'll have to come up with a convincing reason," Phoebe said, scratching absently at a spot on her cheek.

"Maybe we can say that we heard some people talking about taking a few bars and we just want to keep it all secure," Evan said.

"Yeah, that could work," Phoebe agreed.

A few sixth graders came in, and Phoebe was relieved to see that even though the Granville team was down, they were not out. As long as people kept selling boxes, there was hope. Well, as long as people kept selling boxes, they protected their chocolate, and Deerfield didn't blow them out of the water with another prank.

"Let's start putting these away," Phoebe said, heading over to the boxes. She grabbed two and carried them over to the closet, setting them carefully inside.

The others joined her, making an assembly line. Phoebe ended up at the back of the line, the one stacking the boxes inside the closet. It was getting tight, and Phoebe wished she'd brought her protractor to help her create a tessellation where shapes fit perfectly together. There was no space to waste because they really had a lot of boxes yet to sell.

"This is the last one," Evan said, grabbing the final box from the spot on the back wall.

Phoebe craned her neck out to survey the classroom.

"Actually there's another one here," a fifth grader said. The girl walked over to a forgotten box of Sweet and Simples that was sitting on the desk.

"Pass it along," Avery said.

"You know, it looks like it's been opened," the fifth grader said, tugging at the top.

Phoebe froze. Wait. There had not been a box on the desk when she had walked in. And the desk was not part of the assembly line, so there was no reason any of the volunteers would have set it down there. A box should not be opened. And people had been coming in and out. People who could be working for Deerfield.

"No!" Phoebe shouted. She lunged toward the box and tripped over someone's backpack. It was too late. The fifth grader had taken off the lid.

Phoebe instinctively ducked and covered her head, waiting for an explosion that would destroy their chocolate or unleash a plague on all of them. But the room was silent.

Phoebe slowly lowered her arms and stood up. Had it been a false alarm? Everyone was looking at her as though she was out of her mind, so maybe the prank war had finally caught up to her and she'd officially lost it.

But then the fifth grader gagged and covered her nose. The two students nearest to her started coughing and rubbing their eyes. Then all three of them ran from the room.

"Oh, man," Avery said, putting her arm over her nose and mouth. "That is putrid."

"What?" Phoebe asked.

And then the smell hit her. It was worse than the Dumpster at Deerfield. It was worse than her cousin Mark's farts after eating black beans. It was a stench so foul, so rancid, so overpowering that it didn't just stun Phoebe's nose. It assaulted her taste buds, stung her eyes, clogged her lungs, and nearly brought her to her knees.

"Run," Evan called in a choked voice as he staggered out of Granville sales headquarters as though pursued by a flesh-eating monster. And who knew? A smell that vile probably *could* melt flesh. Not that Phoebe was sticking around to find out. She and the remaining volunteers raced out, sputtering, gasping, and choking on the knowledge that yet again Deerfield had bested them.

End of Day Sales Tally: Granville 236, Deerfield 241

CHAPTER 20

TUESDAY, DAY 16

News of the stink bomb had traveled fast. Normally, Gabe would appreciate all the high fives and kudos in the hall, but he was too busy worrying about Julie to be able to enjoy them. Their latest stunt had earned Julie even more popularity, and she had turned further to the dark side. As they walked to sales headquarters together after the final bell, Gabe felt like he was walking with a stranger. A stranger who was eager to get them both jail time.

"I'm thinking we go in for the kill next," Julie said, her eyes glowing as if an alien had taken up residence inside her. Which was probably a possibility that couldn't be ruled out. "They went after all our chocolate, so I say we go after theirs, every last box."

Gabe really did not want to hear how she thought they should commit what would technically be a crime.

"Maybe we should just focus on sales," he said as they walked into room 103.

And then they both stopped because despite the fact that the room was full of volunteers, it was eerily quiet. People were staring at the floor or each other or the ceiling—pretty much anywhere but at Julie and Gabe. It was truly weird.

"What's happening?" Gabe asked, looking around.

For a moment, there was just more silence—clearly no one wanted to tell Gabe and Julie what had taken place.

"What is it?" Julie asked sharply.

And finally Jamal stepped forward. "Our boxes of chocolate—they're gone."

"What do you mean?" Gabe asked, a slow burn starting in the pit of his stomach.

"Did someone move them to the office?" Julie asked. Gabe heard the note of panic in her voice.

"No, we checked," Jamal said.

"Maybe—" Julie began again, but Amber cut her off.

"They're gone, Julie," she said. "Every single box of our chocolate has disappeared."

And now the burn in Gabe's stomach had ignited into an all-out fire.

Julie turned to him. "They did it first," she said in disbelief. "Granville got to our chocolate."

Gabe might not be on the dark side—at least not as far on the dark side as Julie—but there was no way he was taking this. "Well then," he said, his voice deadly as he flexed his fingers. "We'd better go get it back."

CHAPTER 21
TUESDAY, DAY 16

When Phoebe walked into Granville headquarters that afternoon she was shocked to find two fifth graders running out like there was a fire. Meanwhile, several people stood around the desk talking in hushed voices while others gestured angrily. Something was wrong. Something big.

"What's going on?" Phoebe asked.

The moment she spoke, everyone stopped and stared at her. She made eye contact with Avery, but she just shook her head mutely.

"What is it?" Phoebe asked, prickles of anxiety skating up her arms.

Just then the fifth graders who had raced out came back with Evan right behind them.

"What is happening?" Phoebe nearly shouted.

Evan's eyes were flashing, and his fists were balled at his sides. "It's gone," he said.

Phoebe instantly knew what he meant, but she clung to a tiny shred of hope that she was somehow wrong. "Our chocolate?" she asked.

And when he nodded, she felt her own fists ball up.

"Yes," he said. "It's all missing. Every box of every flavor."

They'd done it: Deerfield had finished them off. There was no way Granville could come back from a prank that left their sales supply at zero. Unless they could somehow get it back.

Phoebe was about to say this when her phone vibrated in her pocket.

Evan was already reaching into his own pocket. "Someone's texting me, and it better be an explanation for what's happened to our boxes."

Phoebe fumbled for her phone as well. For a fleeting moment, she remembered that phones were strictly prohibited in school, but this was an emergency.

"I don't believe it," Evan said, his face turning pale.

Phoebe looked down at her phone. There was a text from an unknown number:

If you want to get your chocolate back, come to the community center at 4 p.m.

CHAPTER 22

TUESDAY, DAY 16

Julie's temples throbbed as she and Gabe led their team up the path to the Scottsdale Community Center. Usually she loved coming here. The brick building had a red-and-white Welcome sign on top, and the lobby inside was papered in art projects from student classes and flyers for programs, events, and concerts that took place year-round. It was normally a fun, festive place for the townspeople to come together, not a site where criminals held chocolate for ransom.

The receptionist at the desk took one look at them and, before Julie could open her mouth, pointed down the hall.

"Room seven," he said. "They're waiting for you."

It was impossible not to run, even though the reception-ist called after them to slow down. But now that Granville had done the unthinkable and actually committed the crime of stealing their chocolate, Julie and her team were not slowing down for anything.

Never mind that Julie herself had suggested taking Granville's chocolate—she wouldn't have gone through with it. Well, she might not have. Okay, she would have and why not? The more outrageous her prank ideas had become, the more people came up to her in the halls to tell her how awesome she was. Being the leader doing what it took to win Deerfield both the prank war and the Chocolate Challenge had fully rid Julie of the goody-goody title. It had made her a hero! And now Granville, stupid Granville, was threatening that by robbing Deerfield of their Fantastic Five bars. But it wasn't going to happen—not on co-captain Julie's watch.

The leaders of Granville were waiting for them in the small room with a circle of folding chairs, Phoebe and Evan standing at the front of their group. Seeing them made Julie so angry she thought she might actually froth at the mouth without any prank gum.

"You stole our chocolate!" Julie shouted, striding forward.

Phoebe turned to her, her eyes blazing. "You mean *you* stole *our* chocolate!" she shouted back. "It is not fair—"

"We did not!" Julie cried in outrage, and a few of her volunteers yelled in agreement, making the small room chaotic.

"Yes, you did. Don't lie to us," Evan said sharply.

"I'm tired of you accusing me of awful things!" Julie snapped at Evan.

"You mean tired of me reminding you of awful things you did?" Evan snapped back.

"I already told you a thousand times that I'm sorry I ruined your prank! I'm sorry, I'm sorry, I'm sorry! I didn't mean for everyone at camp to see you in your dumb underwear!" Julie hollered. Then she sucked in her breath. Yikes, had she really just blurted that out?

Yes, she had, because the hectic room had suddenly quieted down considerably and Evan was sending Julie a death glare so searing she could practically feel it burning her flesh.

"No one cares about that," Phoebe said coldly, patting Evan on the back, which made Julie feel even worse at her slipup. "We just care that you stole our chocolate. Well, we got your ransom text saying to meet you here, and we're here. But we're not giving you anything and we want our chocolate back now."

Julie's breath caught in her throat—what was going on?

"But you stole *our* chocolate," Gabe said, his voice now uncertain as he glanced at Julie. "Right?"

Phoebe shook her head. "No . . ." she said, sounding puzzled. "Your chocolate is missing too?"

"Yeah," Julie said. "Our chocolate is gone. We got a text that said to come here if we wanted it back." She hesitated. Were Phoebe and Evan trying to pull the ultimate trick on Deerfield? But they genuinely looked as confused as she felt. She could see some of their teammates whispering to each other, checking to see if anyone was in on the mystery.

"This is crazy," Evan said, his brow crinkled. "Because it means someone not in this room stole *all* the chocolate."

"Who would do that?" Gabe asked.

"And why?" Julie asked, looking around at the other three co-captains.

For the first time since they'd arrived, room 7 was silent because no one had the first clue how to begin answering either of those questions.

CHAPTER 23

TUESDAY, DAY 16

Evan was about to suggest they start a list of possible suspects, though he couldn't actually think of anyone invested in winning the Chocolate Challenge more than the four co-captains already in this room. But just then the doors opened, and two people stepped inside. Evan's stomach turned, and the blood rushed to his head. They were in big, big trouble.

Standing in front of the Deerfield and Granville co-captains and volunteers were their advisors, Mr. Ryan and Ms. Chase, and they did not look pleased to be there.

Mr. Ryan crossed his arms over his chest, and Ms. Chase raised a brow and took a moment to look at each student, one by one.

"Mr. Ryan and I have both gotten some disturbing reports about this year's Chocolate Challenge," Ms. Chase said, when the silence in the room was officially making Evan's skin itch like he still had the horrible spots from the powder. "And we gathered you together to discuss them here, on neutral ground. Does anyone want to hazard a guess as to what those reports might have been?"

Evan stared down at his boots, taking great interest in the melted snow that had pooled under them.

"Did they have anything to do with our chocolate?" Amber asked. "Because it's gone missing."

"It's not missing," Mr. Ryan said shortly. "We've taken it from you. And I think you know why."

Evan heard Amber gulp.

Ms. Chase cleared her throat. "We'll ask again—does anyone have anything to tell us about this year's Chocolate Challenge?"

Evan looked at Phoebe, who for once seemed at a loss for words. Julie's face was turning red as she stared at the floor, and Gabe was tugging on his backpack strap like his life depended on it.

So Evan, his palms damp with cold sweat and his heart pumping like he'd just run a mile, cleared his throat. "Well, we wanted to make the Challenge more fair this year."

Mr. Ryan looked at Evan as though he had lost his mind.

"But things might have gone a little too far," Evan added hastily, his voice squeaky in his ears. He took a step back, nearly bumping into Phoebe.

"Yes, I'd say they did," Ms. Chase said quietly. "They went *way* too far. You riled up small children at a day care, caused a school to shut down for a day, and set off a stink bomb that took hours to clean up."

Evan winced at each item on the list. He'd never considered the fallout from their pranks before.

"And that's only what we know so far," Ms. Chase went on. "I'd imagine these aren't the only incidents that have taken place."

Evan noticed Gabe's cheeks turning pink and Phoebe was blinking extra fast.

"This Challenge is meant to bring our community together," Mr. Ryan said. "But your actions these past few weeks have done the opposite."

"And that's why we are canceling this year's Chocolate Challenge," Ms. Chase said, the words like a smack across Evan's face.

"We can't cancel it," Julie said, her eyes wide. "That would be awful!"

Furious as Evan was with Julie for revealing his summer humiliation, he couldn't help but feel the tiniest bit thankful she had the guts to speak up.

"As awful as pulling a prank at a day care?" Ms. Chase asked, her brows flying up.

Julie bit her lip but then spoke up again. "We made some mistakes, but we did sell a lot of chocolate and—"

"Actually the sales numbers at both schools are at a record low," Mr. Ryan said.

Evan slumped at this news—that was not the record they had hoped to set.

"Apparently you were more focused on jokes than sales," Ms. Chase said. "Which means no one in this room is responsible enough to be a team captain."

"And so we're forced to cancel the Chocolate Challenge, effective immediately," Mr. Ryan said.

With that the two of them walked out.

"Nice job, Julie," Amber said in a poisonous tone, tossing her hair over her shoulder and marching out.

The other volunteers from both schools followed, most either glaring at the four former co-captains, or avoiding looking at them entirely. And a few moments later, it was just Evan, Phoebe, Julie, and Gabe, alone with the bitter knowledge that they were responsible for destroying one of the most celebrated traditions in Scottsdale and denying everyone in town the most delicious chocolate in the world.

CHAPTER 24

TUESDAY, DAY 16

There was nothing Gabe hated more than losing. When his soccer team lost in the playoffs back when Gabe was eight, he'd had such a fit that his dad had had to literally carry him off the field. When his baseball team lost the game that meant they would not be participating in the county championship two years ago, Gabe had written so many letters of protest his coach called his parents in for a meeting. And this fall, when Gabe tripped during a track race, his friend Khai had had to restrain him from preventing other runners from completing the course.

But while each of these losses still needled at Gabe even now, none of them felt as wretched as this one. Okay, maybe things—namely Julie—had gotten a bit out of hand.

But to cancel the entire Challenge? No, that Gabe could not, and would not, accept.

"My parents are going to be so upset when they find out about this," Julie said anxiously. Her shoulders were sagging as though her pink backpack weighed a thousand pounds. For the first time in days she sounded like her old self instead of an evil pranking mastermind.

"Tell me about it," Phoebe said, slumping down in one of the chairs and looking like she would never have the strength to stand again.

"I can't believe they canceled it," Evan said, shaking his head.

And Gabe couldn't believe what wimps they were!

"So you just want to take this lying down," Gabe said. Loudly. So loudly in fact that Evan and Julie started while Phoebe nearly fell off her chair.

"What choice do we have?" Julie asked, pulling at the end of her braid. Gabe couldn't help thinking that all her bravado of the past week had disappeared awfully fast. Though that was probably a good thing: In her ultra-competitive state, who knew what she might have suggested they do?

"You heard what they said," Evan agreed, though Gabe noticed he wasn't looking at Julie. He was probably still upset about the whole underwear thing, a story Gabe would be following up on once the Challenge had been sorted.

Phoebe had recovered from her surprise at Gabe's yelling. "Yeah, it seemed pretty final," she said.

"I can't believe you guys are going to give up so easily," Gabe said, angry at all of them. He began pacing the room, which was suddenly feeling stuffy and small.

"Well, what do you want to do?" Phoebe asked. "Keep selling chocolate even though our supply has been confiscated?"

Gabe stopped pacing and nodded, pleased she had come up with something so fast. "That sounds good," he said, able to speak in a normal tone now that they were getting somewhere.

But Phoebe squinted at him. "I was being sarcastic," she said. "We can't do that."

But Evan drew in a breath. "Actually why can't we do that?" he asked slowly.

"Collect money for chocolate we can't deliver?" Phoebe asked. "Because we don't want to get banished to Antarctica, that's why."

But Evan was starting to smile. "What if we didn't take money?" he said. "What if we just got a bunch of orders and showed Mr. Ryan and Ms. Chase that we *can* be co-captains?"

"That would work," Gabe said. He wasn't fussy about the exact nature of the plan so long as they had a plan.

"I don't know," Julie said. "I mean, what if we couldn't deliver? That would just make everything worse."

Evan glared at her. "So you have a better idea?"

But before she could answer, Phoebe spoke up. "I like the idea of trying to show them that we can handle the Challenge," she said. "Maybe there's something else we could do to convince them?"

"Like what?" Julie asked, clearly still annoyed at Evan's reaction.

"Maybe we could all sign a contract promising not to pull any more pranks?" Phoebe suggested.

"You guys would have to sign a contract promising to stay on your side of town too," Gabe said, casting a dark glare at Evan and Phoebe. "I mean, it's your fault this whole thing started in the first place."

Phoebe put her hands on her hips. "No, it's not," she said. "The whole setup of the contest is unfair, and that's why Deerfield always wins. We just wanted to level the playing field."

Gabe paused at this, but before he could say anything, Julie barreled ahead.

"By cheating?" she asked, raising her eyebrows.

"By taking one of the two big sales so that things were fair for once," Evan retorted.

"I didn't see you complaining last year when you were at Deerfield and we won," Julie said in a sniffy tone.

"That's not the point," Evan said. "The point is that we finally made things even by taking that sale."

Gabe was puzzled—what was Evan talking about?

"Gabe's right. It's your fault this started," Julie said, crossing her arms over her chest. "Because no matter what you call it, taking that sale on our side of town is cheating and we all know it. And you probably just did it to get back at me for what happened at robotics camp this summer, even though I told you a thousand times I was sorry."

"I did not do it to get back at you!" Evan yelled. His face was slowly turning purple. "Though you would have deserved it—and thanks for telling everyone about it today too!"

"So does that mean you'll cheat again if we do this?" Julie roared.

"We didn't cheat the first time!" Phoebe shouted back.

Gabe, who was used to things getting heated on the sidelines of a tough game, put up his hand.

"What did you mean before?" he asked, looking at Phoebe.

The three of them all turned to him.

"You said the contest isn't fair," Gabe explained. "What did you mean?"

Phoebe took what Gabe's mom would call a "calming breath."

"Okay, so the hospital and town hall each buy over fifty bars, right?" she asked.

Gabe glanced at Julie, who nodded despite the fact that her fists were clenched at her sides.

"But the biggest sale on our side never gets more than forty," Phoebe went on. "So Deerfield wins right there, with those numbers. Because there's no making up that deficit."

Gabe and Julie were both silent, considering this.

"She's right," Julie said finally, turning to Gabe.

Much as he was loath to admit it, Gabe knew it was true. He was crazy about winning, but it wasn't much fun winning if the other side didn't have a chance.

"You could have told us, though, instead of just going ahead and selling to the town hall," Julie said to Phoebe.

Phoebe sighed. "Point taken," she said. "I guess we didn't think about how you guys would react."

Julie laughed, surprising Gabe. "I'm sure none of us could have imagined we'd end up here, pariahs of our own town after all the damage we caused."

She had a point.

"I guess I can see why Ms. Chase and Mr. Ryan got so upset," Phoebe admitted grudgingly.

"Yeah, and I'm not sure just signing a contract is going to change their minds," Evan said. "I mean, we shut down school for a day."

"We should still try, though," Julie said. "There has to be *something* we can do to show them we're sorry."

"I have another idea," Phoebe said slowly. "And it just might work. But get ready because it's seriously crazy!"

Gabe grinned—now they were *really* getting somewhere.

CHAPTER 25

WEDNESDAY, DAY 17

Julie glanced at Gabe through the swirling snow. "Do you think we need a bodyguard?" she asked, only half joking.

Gabe laughed but then looked at the building in front of them and grimaced. "I guess we shouldn't exactly expect a warm welcome."

"No, probably not," Julie agreed, looking up at Granville. The final bell had just rung, and students were now streaming out the big metal doors and down the front path toward the sidewalk where Julie and Gabe were standing.

Despite the icy flakes melting on her face and the frigid temperature, Julie was slightly sweaty at the sight of them. Coming here was obviously a bad idea.

But just then two familiar figures appeared on the front steps of the school.

"Julie, Gabe, hurry up!" Phoebe shouted. "It's freezing out here." She and Evan were not wearing coats.

If the students at Granville were as angry at Phoebe and Evan as the students at Deerfield had been at Julie and Gabe today, then inviting the two enemy co-captains into their school was not exactly going to help. But Julie appreciated that they were trying, and she and Gabe hustled up the steps and into the halls of enemy territory. Well, formerly enemy territory.

"Get ready for some death glares," Evan warned them as they began walking against the crowd and deeper into the school. "Ms. Chase made the announcement this morning that the Challenge was canceled, and now pretty much everyone hates us."

"Yeah, it was the same at Deerfield," Julie said, careful to keep her eyes on the floor, something she had gotten very good at earlier in the day. Even if she bumped into something, it was better than facing the anger of her classmates or even worse, Granville students.

"Okay, here we are," Phoebe said, turning the corner and leading them into room 112. "Granville sales headquarters. Though I guess we need a new name now."

Julie sat down in one of the desk chairs, relieved to be

away from the other students. The Granville headquarters was smaller than the one at Deerfield but had the same sad empty space against the back wall where there used to be boxes of Fantastic Five.

"A new name sounds good," Gabe agreed. "What should we call our team?"

Because that's what they were now, a team. At first Julie had been unsure when Phoebe suggested joining forces. After all, the Challenge was meant to be a contest. But given how badly *that* had gone, both schools working together to sell as many boxes as they could and giving the proceeds to both charities was the only thing that made sense. And it was their best shot at getting the Challenge back on, so here they were, four former enemies sitting down to work together.

"We could be the GranFields," Evan suggested as he sat down in the chair that just happened to be the one farthest from Julie.

Julie suppressed a sigh—would he ever get over what had happened at camp? If only she could go back in time to that morning in July when she'd made a series of mistakes that resulted in Evan crashing to the ground, his shorts sliding down to reveal his underwear to the entire camp.

It was the first day of camp, and all the campers had gathered for the big welcome meeting. Julie was sitting up front, of course, and one of the counselors asked her to help out by drawing back the thick curtain from the stage. When Julie tugged back the stage curtain, she'd heard a yelp—unbeknownst to her, Evan was there, setting up a prank, and she'd startled him. He jumped, tripped over a coil of wire that he was evidently going to use, and snagged his shorts on it.

Just as the curtain pulled back, Evan fell out onto the stage—leaving his shorts behind, hooked on the wire. The entire camp witnessed him falling to the ground in his green boxer shorts printed with bananas.

Several campers had caught the incident on their phones, and the video was shown throughout the rest of the week. Evan, a complete laughingstock, had been given the name Banana Butt, just in case he forgot what had happened. Not that he would, obviously. And not that he would ever forget the person who caused the entire debacle in the first place. Julie had apologized a million times, and at this point, what else could she do? Though it probably hadn't helped that she had shouted it out again on Friday. At this rate, Evan would never forgive her.

"No, that sounds too much like grandfathers," Julie said, deciding to ignore Evan. "How about the DeerVilles?"

"Why does Deerfield come first?" Evan asked.

"Because we're the best," Julie said immediately. But

then she noticed Gabe making a face at her. Over the past few days Julie had really tossed off her goody-goody role and gotten amped up over the prank war. But Gabe was right—now was the time to dial that down, not amp it up further. If they wanted to convince Mr. Ryan and Ms. Chase that the Challenge could actually be prank-free, it started here, with the four of them working together.

"Sorry, the DeerVilles are the best," Julie corrected herself.

And now Gabe nodded. "So what's the plan?" he asked.

"I think—" Julie began, just as Phoebe said, "We should—" and Evan said, "Can we—" Then they all laughed.

"This is what happens when four co-captains try to work together," Julie said.

"Four bossy co-captains," Phoebe added with a grin. "Who all know how to get things done."

"Working together was your idea, so you should start," Julie said, figuring fair was fair.

"Thanks," Phoebe said, smiling at Julie. It felt weird to have Phoebe smile at her after weeks of being sworn enemies. But it was a good weird. In fact Julie thought she could actually see herself being friends with Phoebe.

"I think the first thing to do is tell Ms. Chase and Mr. Ryan that we're united now—that the prank war is over and we're all going to focus on selling as many boxes of Fantastic Five as we can," Phoebe said.

"Maybe even a record-setting amount," Gabe put in, sounding more excited about that than the working together part of things.

"Definitely a record-setting amount," Evan agreed. "We'll show them that together Team DeerVille can blow past sales numbers out of the water."

Gabe was grinning at that, and Julie had to admit it sounded good, even though it was Evan's idea and he still wouldn't look in her direction.

"We should find out the highest number of sales ever so we can beat it," Phoebe said, going over to one of the computers.

"And then we should find Ms. Chase to convince her we can do this," Evan said.

While Phoebe was looking up the number, Julie pulled out a surprise: four of the Triple Crown bars from the supply of boxes her family had bought. She figured any meeting with chocolate had to go well. "Does anyone want one?" she asked, holding them up.

"That's the dumbest question anyone's ever asked me," Gabe said with a grin, taking a bar for himself and passing two others to Evan and Phoebe.

Julie laughed as she unwrapped her bar, then breathed in the exquisite scent of the Triple Crown. She bit into it, the sweet shell giving way to the decadent liquid center, the fudge buttery rich as it melted in her mouth. Was there anything better on the planet?

"Okay, I have the sales number," Phoebe said, looking at the computer screen once they had finished their chocolate. "The most boxes ever sold was two years ago, when together both schools sold nine hundred and twelve."

"We can beat that, easy," Gabe said, waving his hand as if that number was nothing.

"Actually, how many boxes have we sold so far?" Julie asked.

Phoebe turned back to the computer and a minute later turned back to them, her nose scrunched. "Only four hundred and seventy-seven," she said. "And there are only fourteen days left of the Challenge."

"If we can even convince the teachers to let us have a Challenge," Evan added.

"We can," Julie said firmly, standing up. "Let's go find Ms. Chase right now."

She headed out of the room, the other members of the DeerVille team following.

CHAPTER 26

WEDNESDAY, DAY 17

"No," Ms. Chase said the moment they walked into her classroom.

Phoebe stumbled over her own boots, and Julie, who was next to her, grabbed her elbow so that she didn't fall. This was not the reception Phoebe had been hoping for.

Part of Phoebe was ready to turn right around. But Julie's firm grip on her elbow gave her just enough courage to try.

"Ms. Chase, we know how badly we messed up," she began. "And we're sorry. Truly."

"I'm glad to hear it," Ms. Chase said briskly. She was stacking copies of *Where the Red Fern Grows* and did not look up. "But it doesn't change anything. The Challenge is canceled, end of story."

Phoebe had somehow not realized it would be this hard, and judging from the way Evan had his hands squeezed together, Julie was pulling at the end of her braid, and Gabe was slouching, they likely felt the same. So Phoebe tried again.

"We actually came here to introduce ourselves," she said in a strong voice. Okay, it shook a little, but hopefully it wasn't noticeable.

"To introduce yourselves?" Ms. Chase asked. The good news was that she had finally looked up from book stacking. The bad news was that she clearly thought Phoebe had lost her mind. "We've met."

"Well, you've met us as individuals and as co-captains of two different teams, Deerfield and Granville," Julie jumped in, and Phoebe could have hugged her for knowing just what Phoebe was thinking.

"But that's in the past," Evan said, starting to grin. "Today we're a new team."

"The DeerVilles!" Gabe concluded with a fist pump.

Ms. Chase's mouth had dropped open, so Phoebe forged ahead. "We're a team of four co-captains uniting two schools to sell more boxes of chocolate than have ever been sold before."

"And to raise money for two charities, not just one," Evan added.

Ms. Chase closed her mouth but remained speechless.

"We're going to make you and our schools and the whole town proud," Julie said. "If you'll just give us the chance."

And now all four of them waited for Ms. Chase to speak. The silence was so silent it was loud in Phoebe's ears. Or maybe that was just the sound of her heart beating extra hard as Ms. Chase weighed their fate.

"I appreciate your desire to make the Challenge something we can all be proud of," Ms. Chase said finally, crossing her arms over her chest. "But I'm not sure you realize the damage you inflicted. It took teachers at Dandelion Day Care ages to soothe the kids after Julie left."

Phoebe saw Evan duck his head at this.

"And the stink bomb here probably seemed funny to you, but it was a lot of work for the janitors to clear out the room afterward. Mr. Samuels and Mr. Claiborne had to stay late."

Gabe seemed to shrink a bit hearing that.

"And I'm sure it was exciting that Deerfield got a day off because of the thermostat," Ms. Chase said.

Now Phoebe was looking down at her boots to avoid the teacher's gaze.

"We have an extra snow day to spare, so there won't be the expense and inconvenience of losing a vacation day," Ms. Chase went on.

That hadn't even occurred to Phoebe as a possibility, and she shuddered at the thought of how bad it could have been.

"But a number of the administrators had to come in and work in the cold, overseeing the heat coming back on and maintaining the business of the day," Ms. Chase said. "In their coats and gloves."

Phoebe glanced at Evan, who looked as though he'd swallowed rocks. Which was pretty much how Phoebe felt.

"We're sorry," Evan began, but Ms. Chase shook her head.

"I appreciate that," their faculty advisor said. "But in this case, sorry and good intentions simply aren't enough. The Challenge is off, and that's final."

With that, Ms. Chase walked out of the room, taking any hopes Team DeerVille had of reviving the Challenge with her. Scottsdale wouldn't be having a sweet holiday season, and it was all Phoebe's fault.

CHAPTER 27

SUNDAY, DAY 21

Sunday afternoon the doorbell rang while Evan was up in his bedroom finishing his math homework. He was stuck on the last problem and about to call Phoebe—who was not only good at doing math, she was good at explaining it—when he heard a knock at his door.

"Come in," he called, and a moment later, the last person in the world he expected to see walked in. "Julie," Evan said, his phone slipping out of his hand.

She strode through the door, her brown hair back in its usual braid, her cheeks pink from the chilly wind blowing through Scottsdale.

"Actually I have my blowfish underwear on today," Julie said.

Evan was taken aback and slightly horrified by this unnecessary revelation. He was also unsure why she had shared it. He knew she liked winning—had losing the Challenge pushed her over the edge?

Julie carefully placed her phone next to him at the desk, set it to video, and pressed record.

Clearly she had truly lost it.

"Um," Evan began. He had absolutely no idea what to say next.

"So you and everyone watching this can call me Blowfish Butt," she said in a crisp voice, looking straight at the phone that was now filming her.

Before Evan could react, Julie took a step forward, flailed her arms, gave a loud yell, and, looking completely ridiculous, crumpled to the floor.

Evan was speechless.

Julie stood up and brushed herself off, then picked up her phone, and turned off her video. "So now we have a video where I look stupid and I even give myself an embarrassing nickname. Right?"

Evan nodded.

Julie was messing with her phone. "And now I'm sending it to you. I wanted to make this video for you because—"

"I know why you did it," Evan interrupted as his phone pinged with the video she'd sent. "You wanted to make up for the whole Banana Butt thing at camp." Just saying the detested nickname made Evan slightly nauseous. Though interestingly not as nauseous as it usually did.

"Yeah," Julie said, putting her phone down. "I figured that since you didn't believe me when I said sorry, I had to show you. Though I'm not going to show you my underwear because that would just be wrong."

Evan nodded fiercely at that.

"Okay, you have the video and you can send it to anyone you want," Julie said, sitting down at his desk chair. "So does that mean you will finally forgive me?"

Evan waited, but the familiar hot, itchy anger he felt every time he'd seen Julie since camp was not there. Which surprised him because it had seemed so permanent. But somehow her willingness to go this far to get his forgiveness—to look that dumb just for him—had cooled the anger and reshaped it into something new. Something a lot like forgiveness.

So Evan shrugged and smiled. "You're willing to be Blowfish Butt for me—how could I not forgive you?"

He was surprised to see Julie actually get a bit teary at this. Although maybe it shouldn't surprise him. After all, she was willing to look ridiculous to get him to forgive her—it obviously meant more to her than he'd realized.

"Okay, good," Julie said. "I'm really sad we lost the Challenge, but at least you and I are friends again."

Evan froze. They were friends again because Julie had *showed* him she was sorry. She'd said it a million times, but it wasn't until she had done something to try to make it better that he had truly believed her.

"I have an idea," Evan said slowly. "And I think it might be a good idea."

"What?" Julie asked, tipping her head and waiting.

"I have to tell everyone at once," Evan said, picking up his phone to text Phoebe and Gabe. "We need an emergency meeting of the DeerVilles."

"But the DeerVilles are over," Julie said, her tone wistful.

"Not necessarily," Evan said, starting to text. "Not necessarily."

CHAPTER 28

MONDAY, DAY 22

Julie kept her head down as she and Gabe navigated the hostile halls of Deerfield. All Julie wanted to do was head home—it had been a long day of snotty comments and death glares. Everyone at Deerfield was still good and mad about the canceled Challenge, and they were not shy about blaming Julie and Gabe. Though of course they had a point.

But it was Julie's hope that Evan, who was coming to meet them at the side door of the school with Phoebe, had come up with the idea that would save the contest. She didn't know what the idea was, but in just a few minutes, she'd find out.

Gabe was at the side door when she arrived. They had realized that the co-captains of Granville showing up at Deerfield might induce a riot, so this was their solution: sneak Evan and Phoebe in the side of the school while everyone else was heading out the front. It was the sort of thing Julie had read famous people did when avoiding the paparazzi. Though in their case, it was more about avoiding people who might want to egg them instead of taking their picture.

"I think I see them," Gabe said, gazing out. Julie peeked over his shoulder, and sure enough she saw Evan in his red wool hat and Phoebe with her turquoise-and-plum scarf hurrying toward them.

"Tell me we won't run into anyone else who hates us today," Phoebe said as they came inside, stamping their boots to clear them of snow.

Julie shook her head. "I wish I could," she said, shivering a bit and glad when the door closed behind them. "Bad day?"

"The worst," Phoebe said, sighing as they headed down the empty hall toward room 103. "I think people are even angrier at us today than they were last week."

"Same," Gabe said. Even his wild hair seemed subdued today. "Today at lunch my friend Joe brought Fantastic

Five bars for everyone but me—he said he didn't have enough because the Challenge was canceled."

"Well, I think I have an idea that might fix things," Evan said as they reached the safety of Deerfield sales head-quarters and closed the door firmly behind them.

Room 103 had already begun transforming back into a regular classroom. Only one computer was left and the desks had been moved into groups, not the circle they had been. Seeing it made Julie's chest tight.

"Let's hear the big idea," Phoebe said, sitting down at one of the desks in a group of four and looking at Evan.

"Okay, so yesterday Julie came to my house," Evan began as the rest of them sat down. "And she—" He looked at her. "Can I tell them?"

Sure," she said. She had to admit she was kind of proud she'd finally figured out how to get Evan to forgive her. Well, in fairness it was her mom who had given her the idea. When she saw Julie moping over the weekend, she'd asked what was going on. Julie couldn't admit to the can-celation of the Challenge—not yet and hopefully not ever—so she told her mom the other thing that was bother-ing her, which was how much Evan hated her. And her mom had suggested the "don't tell him, show him" approach. Which had worked like a charm. Her mom could be annoying about things like bedtime and eating green vegetables, but when things were really grim, she came through.

"Julie made a video of herself where she looked almost as ridiculous as I did at summer camp," Evan said.

Phoebe perked up. "We never did get that whole camp story," she said eagerly.

Evan raised a brow at her. "And you never will," he said. "The Banana Butt incident is never to be mentioned again. The point is that Julie made me look like a fool, so to apologize she made a video of herself looking stupid for me to show everyone."

Now it was Gabe who perked up. "Great, where's the video?"

Julie looked at Evan and rolled her eyes at the density of their co-captains. "Guys, you're missing the point," she said, resisting the urge to pinch them both.

"Wow, he really did forgive you if you guys are on the same side on something," Phoebe said.

"Yeah, I never thought that would happen," Gabe agreed. He had picked up a pen that was on the desk and tapped it against one palm.

Okay, well, now they were on the road to getting it.

"Right," Evan continued, "so the point is that Julie told me she was sorry a million times, but it wasn't until she showed me she was sorry that I forgave her."

"I still want to see that video of Julie, though," Gabe said, tapping the pen harder.

Julie reached over and snatched the pen, frustrated. "No video," she snapped. "And a little more listening please."

"Jeez," Gabe muttered, but finally settled down.

"Evan, go ahead," Julie said.

"Right, so what I'm thinking is—"

"That Ms. Chase didn't get how sorry we were because we just told her," Phoebe interrupted. "So if we want to get the contest back on, we need to show her we're sorry. Evan, you're a genius!"

"Well, maybe," Evan said with a grin. "With Julie's help."

"We make a good team, but I think you get credit for this," Julie said. She was also impressed with Evan. It was more than a good idea; it was a revelation. "It's so smart I can't believe we didn't realize it before—so where do we start? I think we should call Dandelion Day Care and offer to come in and read to the kids before nap time or something. And maybe we could help out the janitors at Granville after school one day, to make up for the stink bomb?"

"Does she always answer her own questions?" Phoebe asked Gabe and Evan.

"Yes," they replied in exact unison.

They looked at each other and laughed along with Phoebe.

Julie rolled her eyes, but then she laughed too. The laughter didn't feel mean now. "I got excited, sorry," she said.

"No, don't be sorry," Phoebe said. "Your answers are spot-on. And what should we do for the administrators who had to come in and work through the cold day here?"

"Maybe we could answer phones and do filing for an hour so they could have an extra coffee break?" Julie asked.

"Sounds good," Phoebe agreed, leaning back in her seat. "We could also pool our money and buy chocolate bars for all of them and the janitors."

"Oh, good thinking," Evan agreed. "Nothing inspires forgiveness like chocolate."

Julie agreed with that—and wished that one of them had brought some Fantastic Five bars for the meeting. A silky Sweet and Simple or her beloved Triple Crown, with its rich dark chocolate shell, would really hit the spot right now.

"There's just one problem, though," Phoebe said, twisting the end of her scarf. "Doing all that is going to take a few days and there are only nine days left of the Challenge. If we take the time to show everyone we're sorry, and do it right, there won't be enough time to sell many boxes."

Gabe sat up straight. "And then we wouldn't break the record. I say we start selling now, today."

"But Ms. Chase said not to," Julie said, her stomach suddenly beginning to swirl uncomfortably.

"Yeah, but once we do this, I'm sure Ms. Chase and Mr. Ryan will say the Challenge is back on," Gabe said dismissively.

"I think that's true," Phoebe said thoughtfully. "And we could do both things at once."

"Ms. Chase told us not to, though," Julie repeated, tugging on the end of her braid as her stomach swirled faster. "And it's not like it went well the first time we started breaking the rules."

For a moment, no one spoke because there was no arguing with that. And in that silence, Julie thought about how good it had felt to consider doing something that was, well, good. Figuring out how to fix a problem according to the rules—that did not make Julie feel as if she was going to puke. But getting back into the territory of rule breaking was like turning on a blender in the pit of her belly. And for the first time Julie realized how out of sorts amping up her competitive side had made her feel.

"I think this might be different," Phoebe said slowly, lacing her fingers together. "Because, yeah, we'd be going against what a teacher said, but we'd be doing it for a good reason."

"That's true," Evan agreed. "I mean, everyone wants this Challenge, not just us, and while it would be awesome if we beat that record"—Gabe nodded enthusiastically at this—"it's not like we're going to break any rules to make it happen. We're just going to sell chocolate."

"And chocolate is always good," Phoebe added with a grin. "It'll make people happy."

What they said made sense, but it did nothing to settle Julie's spinning stomach. "When would we tell the teachers what we were doing?" she asked, pressing a hand against her middle.

"How about just as soon as we show our apologies to everyone?" Phoebe suggested. "And by the way, is there a word for that?"

"Reparations," Julie said automatically. "That's when you try to make up for a bad action by doing something good."

"Which is exactly what this would be," Evan said, leaning back in his chair and stretching a little. "And if we do one place a day and start today, we'll be done by Wednesday afternoon. So we can tell Ms. Chase and Mr. Ryan Thursday."

"Which means we will only be doing secret sales for three days," Phoebe said to Julie. "Does that sound all right?"

Julie wanted to agree, but the words wouldn't come, maybe because of the way her stomach was now a whirlpool.

"Julie, we won't do it if you don't want to." It was Gabe who spoke, surprising Julie. "If you're more comfortable waiting, we will."

"Or the three of us could do sales, but you could wait until we have the official okay," Phoebe added.

That was what Julie wanted, rather desperately in fact, but that made her stomach hurt in a whole new way. "Does it make me a goody-goody that I want to wait until we have permission?" she whispered.

Gabe patted her arm. "Yes," he said.

Julie slumped down in her seat.

"Gabe!" Phoebe snapped reproachfully.

"Well, it does," Gabe said. "But so what? You *are* a goody-goody, so own it. Honestly I think it's a good thing. I mean, that's how you get great grades."

"And scholarships to camps," Evan added, nodding. "And elected to be co-captain of everything you can co-captain."

"And it's how you come up with awesome ideas for reparations," Phoebe said with a grin.

"And it's how we know what reparations even are," Gabe said. "So yeah, you're a goody-goody, but that's cool. Go with it."

"Be you," Evan added, and Phoebe nodded.

Julie felt herself starting to smile because maybe, just maybe, her friends were right. Well, they were definitely right about Julie being a goody-goody. Her time trying to prove she wasn't had only proven how much of a goody-goody she actually was. But maybe they were right about the other part too—maybe it *was* a good thing. Julie liked getting top grades and being elected co-captain and knowing what words like "reparations" meant. So maybe instead of trying to change it, it was time to own it, as Gabe had said. And be proud of who she was instead of stressing about what people like Amber might say.

"So I should just be my goody-goody self and not worry about it," Julie said.

"Yup," Evan said, giving her a thumbs-up.

"And let's face it, you were scary when you went over to the dark side," Gabe said, shuddering rather dramatically. "You made me look non-competitive you were so hard-core."

Julie laughed. "I think I take things to the extreme," she said.

Evan snickered. "You could say that."

"So take the whole goody-goody thing to extremes," Phoebe said. "And you'll end up running the world."

Julie did rather like the sound of that.

And so as the DeerVille co-captains planned the way that four of them would make reparations and three of them would begin secret sales, Julie accepted her innate goody-goody side and got ready to rule the world. Or at least rule *her* world.

CHAPTER 29

MONDAY, DAY 22

"So you're seriously never going to tell us what Banana Butt means?" Gabe asked Evan as they trooped down Spruce Street. The Arctic wind was whipping up swirls of snow that stung Gabe's cheeks, and he pulled his hat down low.

Gabe and Evan, along with two Triple Crown bars Julie had in her bag, were heading to find the Granville janitors while Phoebe gathered supplies for a sale and Julie went to hunt down more chocolate bars for the administrators of Deerfield.

Evan scuffed his boots in the crunchy sidewalk snow. "You're not going to stop asking me about it, are you?"

"No, definitely not and you know Phoebe's never letting it go," Gabe said hopefully. "So you might as well just get it over with." Evan seemed to consider this as they crossed Blossom Boulevard, but just then Gabe caught site of several Deerfield students, including Amber, on the other side. "We should hurry," he told Evan.

But it was too late—they had been spotted.

"So no one at your own school will hang out with you now, right?" Amber called as both Evan and Gabe picked up their pace.

"I guess traitors stick together," a fifth grader shouted as they rounded the corner of Hazel.

"I think I know how Wolverine felt before he met up with the other X-Men," Evan said.

Gabe really liked this analogy except for one thing. "I think I'm more like Wolverine," he said. "You're more like Cyclops."

"I don't even wear glasses," Evan said.

They'd reached Granville, so Gabe decided to pick up the conversation later—right after he found out the Banana Butt story. But first things first.

Gabe followed Evan through the halls, feeling thankful the students of Granville were either in after-school clubs or had left for the day. The janitors' workroom was next to the cafeteria, and Gabe was glad to see several of them were inside.

"Hi, we're looking for Mr. Claiborne and Mr. Samuels," Evan said as they walked in. The room was infused with the sharp scent of pine cleaner that sat in buckets along the back wall.

"You found us," a tall man with a deep voice said. "I'm Mr. Claiborne and this is Mr. Samuels." He tipped his head toward a man standing by the back closet drinking a soda.

"Well, unless someone just threw up—then we have no idea where those men are," Mr. Samuels said with a smile.

Gabe had to laugh at that.

"No, sir, no puke," Evan said. "We're here because we're responsible for the stink bomb the other day, and we wanted to apologize by volunteering to help out this afternoon."

Both janitors stopped looking so friendly when the stink bomb was mentioned.

"And to give you these," Gabe said quickly, pulling the Triple Crowns out of his pocket, hoping the chocolate would help. Sure enough, both men smiled again as Gabe gave them the bars. Chocolate really could work miracles.

"We're serious about helping you out," Evan said, taking off his jacket.

The room was warm, so Gabe slid his off too.

"We only have one thing left to do this afternoon," Mr. Samuels said slowly. "But if you do want to help, you're going to need to put those jackets back on."

Ten minutes later, Gabe and Evan stood outside the side door of Granville wishing they had brought masks. Or the nose plugs swimmers wore. That was because despite the cold weather, the Granville cafeteria Dumpster smelled like a rank mix of moldy meat loaf, rotten broccoli, and decaying bananas. It was so bad Gabe's eyes were actually watering.

"You sure you boys are up to the job?" Mr. Claiborne asked heartily.

Gabe was not sure at all. When he pictured helping out the janitors, it had been in a classroom watering plants or refilling paper towel dispensers, not cleaning out the cafeteria Dumpster after the trash was taken away. But he and Evan had volunteered: There was no backing out now.

"Yes, sir," Gabe said.

"Well, thanks, boys, this is a nice thing you're doing," Mr. Samuels said.

"We just hope it makes up for the stink bomb," Evan said. He was already pulling on the big rubber gloves they'd been given.

The two men nodded and headed into the warm, stink-free school, leaving Gabe and Evan on their own. Gabe gazed at the big green rectangular monstrosity that wafted the most disgusting scent he had ever smelled.

"Do we have to actually get inside the Dumpster?" Evan asked in a slightly strangled voice, like he was trying to block off his nose from the inside.

"I don't see how else we can clean the sides like they said," Gabe said, looking at the mop-like scrub brushes and bucket of cleaner they'd been given. "But I wish there was."

"I think we need hazmat suits," Evan said, climbing up the ladder that leaned against the Dumpster, which was the size of a backyard shed, his entire face scrunching up as he viewed the inside.

"Or X-Men powers that shut off your sense of smell," Gabe said, following him with the cleaning supplies.

The smell inside the Dumpster was even worse.

"We have to text the girls about this," Gabe said, pulling his phone out of his pocket. "So that they appreciate how we're suffering for the team."

"Wait, send proof or they won't believe it," Evan said. They picked up the scrub brushes and took a quick selfie; then Gabe set up a group text and sent it to all of them.

"I don't think I'll ever eat again," Evan said as they both dipped their scrub brushes in the bucket and got started on opposite sides of the Dumpster.

Gabe gagged as he stepped on something soft that squashed under his boot. "We're going to need full decontamination after this."

"Seriously," Evan agreed.

They scrubbed the metal walls of the Dumpster down quickly and were just tossing the brushes and empty bucket over the side when Evan let out a shriek.

Gabe wanted to laugh at the sound, but the stricken look on Evan's face stopped him.

"I heard something," Evan said, looking around wildly. "Like an animal scratching."

And just then it came again. It sounded like claws scraping at the far corner of the Dumpster. Gabe looked over, then recoiled at the small whiskered face with beady eyes staring hungrily back at him. A rat. It was just like the scariest movie he'd ever seen: *Radioactive Rat Attack*. It had even started a lot like this, two innocent people and one evil rat trapped together in a small space.

"Run!" Gabe shouted, rushing toward the ladder. But in his haste, he slipped on the wet floor of the Dumpster. Evan, who was also charging toward the ladder, tripped over Gabe. They both yelled as the creature ran toward them, claws scratching at the metal floor.

"We're going to die!" Gabe screeched, struggling to get to his feet but slipping and falling a second time. He curled up on the bottom of the Dumpster, readying for a bite from the rat, which was most likely rabid, just like in *Radioactive Rat Attack*.

"Um, Gabe," Evan said a moment later.

Gabe opened his eyes and saw Evan standing over him, offering a hand up.

"It turns out it was just a mouse," Evan said. "And I think it was a lot more scared of us than we were of it."

Gabe was not so sure about that, but he uncurled from his fetal position on the bottom of the Dumpster.

"Listen," he said as Evan helped him up. "That was probably the most humiliating thing that has ever happened to me and you saw it."

Evan did not deny this.

"So now you really have to tell me the Banana Butt story so we can be even," Gabe finished.

Evan laughed. "Okay," he said as they started up the ladder. "I guess after this I can definitely trust you to keep it a secret."

That was for sure.

"And Phoebe will too," Evan continued. "I'll tell you guys but only in a completely secure location."

"And we'll never speak of this Dumpster disaster again, right?" Gabe confirmed.

"Roger that," Evan said with a grin. "Well, we have to tell the girls."

"Yeah, but I meant besides them," Gabe said. Obviously they'd tell Phoebe and Julie.

Once they were finally outside the Dumpster, Gabe looked at Evan and started to laugh. "You have orange peel stuck to your jacket," he said.

Evan looked at Gabe and snickered. "I think you have three candy bar wrappers stuck to yours."

As Gabe reached to pull off the wrappers they heard footsteps. A moment later, Phoebe and Julie appeared from around the corner of the building.

"Wow, you guys are foul," Julie said, covering her face.

"We know," Gabe told her.

"Believe me, we know," Evan added, pulling off the peel and making Phoebe shriek in disgust.

"It's a good thing we came, then," Julie said, pulling her backpack off her shoulder. "We brought supplies." She pulled out a bottle of hand sanitizer and two Fantastic Five bars.

"We figured this was the only way to say thanks for taking a hit for our team," Phoebe said, picking up one of the now filthy scrub brushes. "We have to bring these back inside, right?"

Julie gathered up the other brush and bucket while Evan helped himself to half the bottle of sanitizer, then held it out to Gabe.

Gabe looked at the three of them. This was what it meant to be a team. It was the guy who had your back when you fell on the floor of a Dumpster and didn't make fun of you for being scared of a mouse. It was Julie and Phoebe showing up with sanitizer and chocolate and helping out with the last step of a truly disgusting job, not because they had to but because they didn't want their teammates to do it alone. *This* was what people meant when they said that being part of a team mattered more than winning. And for the first time ever, Gabe realized it was true.

"Gabe, are you okay?" Julie asked, her brows crinkling.

Gabe cleared his throat. "Yeah, of course," he said, taking the sanitizer. He certainly wasn't going to get all mushy or anything. He still wanted to set the record and be part of the best Challenge in the history of Scottsdale—that was a given.

But as they walked into Granville, Gabe had to admit

that being part of this team truly did mean more than a win ever could.

"Good news," he said as they walked down the hall. "Evan's finally spilling the Banana Butt story."

Evan groaned, Phoebe cheered, and Julie laughed.

Yeah, this was Gabe's team, and while a win would be awesome, being on this team was better than anything.

CHAPTER 30

TUESDAY, DAY 23

Phoebe could hear the happy shrieks and giggles of the Dandelion Day Care toddlers before she and Julie had even walked up the steps of the school. Today she and Julie were on reparations duty while the boys were off doing their first secret sale.

"The kids sound so cute," she said to Julie.

"Yeah," Julie said somewhat warily. "Though they were surprisingly loud when I was there last time."

The porch of the school had a cheery red mat that Phoebe used to stomp the snow off her boots. "That was probably just the gum," she said. "I bet they'll be totally sweet as long as we don't start frothing."

Julie snickered as they knocked on the door of the

center. She heard footsteps and then Ms. Fahadi opened it and waved them inside.

"Thank you so much for giving us this chance to make things up to you," Julie said as they walked in.

"I wasn't sure when you called," Ms. Fahadi admitted. She was wearing green pants and a soft brown sweater. "But we certainly try to teach the kids that everyone makes mistakes and that you can learn important things from those mistakes."

"We definitely made a mistake," Phoebe said, looking at the cubbies that had bright little boots and fuzzy little jackets sticking out. She was utterly charmed and could not wait to meet the darlings who wore these teensy clothes. She'd always wanted a little sister, and this afternoon was as close as she'd probably ever get.

"And everyone deserves a second chance," Ms. Fahadi said. "Plus the timing was ideal. Miss Jane called in sick this week, so we can use the extra help."

Julie appeared slightly worried at this news, but Phoebe thought it was great—it made their reparations even better.

"I'm so glad we can be of service," Phoebe said as she and Julie hung up their jackets and backpacks on the adult coat rack.

"You'll be reading to the Tigers," Ms. Fahadi said, leading them down a hallway with a rainbow rug and more kid art on the walls. "That's the four-year-olds. They've been told you're coming for story hour, and they're excited."

Phoebe was nearly skipping as Ms. Fahadi turned into the Tigers' room, but as soon as she stepped inside, she stopped. Excited seemed to be a bit of an understatement. The kids were running around like there was an actual tiger set loose and chasing them. She looked at Julie, who nodded knowingly.

"All right, Tigers, show me your best roar," Ms. Fahadi said, and a moment later, Phoebe was ready to run for cover as the room exploded in wild growls and straight-up screams.

"Wonderful," Ms. Fahadi told the children warmly. Clearly she'd already gone deaf from past demonstrations because Phoebe's ears were ringing.

"Phoebe and Julie, this is Miss Emma, the head teacher of the Tigers," Ms. Fahadi said.

"Welcome," Miss Emma said, with an understandably tired-looking smile. Her blond hair was back in a ponytail that was coming loose, and her jeans had two small handprints on the back, in what appeared to be pink paint. "The kids have been looking forward to meeting you. Why don't you pick out a few books to read and I'll get the kids ready?"

"Sounds good," Phoebe said. She was lying, though—it did not sound good at all because she could not imagine this raucous group quieting for a moment, let alone the ten minutes it would take to read a book. But she nonetheless selected a book about dinosaurs—her favorite when she was young—and waited as Miss Emma clapped three times in an attempt to get the group's attention.

"Okay, Tigers, let's sit in a circle on the rug for story time," she said. This produced what appeared to be a riot, with ten four-year-olds shoving, yelling, and pushing their way to the orange-and-black-striped rug at the back of the room.

Phoebe winced as a particularly rambunctious girl stepped on her foot while racing for a spot next to Miss Emma.

"Miss Phoebe and Miss Julie are going to read you stories today," Miss Emma said. "Miss Phoebe, will you begin?"

"Sure," Phoebe said, pushing her mouth into a smile as she sat on the small chair next to Miss Emma.

The kids were in a lopsided circle and two were lying down instead of sitting, but the noise level had gone down considerably, and when Phoebe held up the book, almost all of them looked at her.

Phoebe cleared her throat. "This is a book about—"

"How old are you?" a boy with messy brown hair shouted.

"I'm—" Phoebe started.

"I hate that book!" a girl in a pink dress screeched, kicking her feet on the rug.

"Miss Emma, Jill said 'hate' and we don't say 'hate' in school," a boy with black curls whined.

Jill reached over and smacked the boy who had tattled.

Phoebe winced and looked at Julie, who had taken a step back and was holding her chosen book in front of her like a shield.

Both kids screamed as Miss Emma spoke calmly about a "time-out table" and "keeping our hands to ourselves." When the mess was sorted, she turned back to Phoebe and nodded.

"This is a book about dinosaurs," Phoebe began again. And this time she was able to start—and finish—the story.

Julie read her book next, and then Miss Emma announced it was nap time. Phoebe kind of wished she could curl up on one of the cots along the side wall because she could not remember ever being so exhausted. These kids were wild! She could not even imagine how hard it must have been to settle them down after Julie's frothing gum.

Phoebe felt a sticky hand grab her own, and she looked

down. Jill, in her rumpled pink dress, looked up at Phoebe. "Do you want to see my cot?"

"Sure," Phoebe said, her heart squeezing as the small girl pulled Phoebe to a cot covered with a pink blanket.

"This is my monkey," Jill told Phoebe, holding up a stuffed monkey with ratty fur and a missing ear. "Her name is Monkey."

"Great name," Phoebe said, remembering that she had once had a lamb named Lamb.

"You can tuck me in," Jill announced, getting onto her cot and kicking at the blanket.

"I can help, but shouldn't you take your shoes off first?" Phoebe asked as she gathered the blanket.

"They're new," Jill explained, holding up a foot so that Phoebe could see the pink sneakers with Velcro.

"They're very pretty," Phoebe said. She wasn't sure it was okay for Jill to sleep in them, but she'd seen Jill angry and was not interested in seeing it again, so she just fluffed the blanket over her, sneakers and all.

"They help me run very fast," Jill said.

"Okay, well, have a good sleep," Phoebe said, smoothing down Jill's blanket. Around them, other kids were settled on their cots and hugging their own stuffed animals or dolls.

"No," Jill said.

Phoebe bit her lip. Was Jill going to start screaming again?

"If I go to sleep, you'll go away," Jill argued, grabbing Phoebe's arm with her sticky fingers and holding on tight.

Phoebe could not help feeling flattered. "I do have to go," she said.

"It's not fair," Jill sulked, the words so familiar to Phoebe she smiled.

"I can come another day and visit," she said.

"But that's not today," Jill stated logically. "So it's not fair."

Phoebe saw Jill's point. But she saw more too. And she realized something: Maybe "fair" was something she had never fully understood before the Challenge and the prank war and the forming of the DeerVilles. And that maybe, after all that, she got it just a little bit more.

"Jill, do you like math?" she asked, sitting down on the edge of Jill's cot.

"What's math?" Jill asked.

Right, she was four. "Well, it's like if you have one carrot and then you get another carrot, you have two carrots."

"I don't like carrots," Jill said, rolling over on her side but keeping a tight hold on Phoebe's arm.

"Okay, but math is really cool," Phoebe said. "I promise you'll like math when you get older. And one of the best parts of math is variables."

Jill was now sucking her thumb, but her eyes were still on Phoebe.

"Variables are unknowns," Phoebe told her. "And when they're part of an equation, all kinds of things can happen."

Phoebe looked around for Julie and saw that she was sitting on a chair in the dress-up area listening to Phoebe. Phoebe smiled at her. Julie had been a very important variable lately.

"Do varies make bad things happen?" Jill asked, the words muffled over her thumb.

Phoebe thought about the prank war. "Sometimes variables can lead to mistakes," she said. "But mistakes can be good if you learn from them."

Phoebe glanced up at Julie, who gave her a knowing look because they had both definitely made a few mistakes these past few weeks, but as Ms. Fahadi had said, you could learn a lot from a mistake.

"And sometimes something that seems unfair can actually even out in unexpected ways," Phoebe told Jill, thinking out loud. "Sometimes when you first see an equation with variables, you think you know what it means. You think you know the answer before you even start to work on the problem."

Like how Phoebe had thought the answer to the uneven contest was to even it with a single sale outside their territory. Or that the answer to one prank was another.

Jill's eyes were closing, and Miss Emma had turned down the lights.

"But the fantastic thing about math," Phoebe concluded quietly. "Is that you don't always know—because sometimes a variable can be the best surprise you could ever imagine."

A variable like pranks that turned nemeses into new friends and joined two teams together to be one.

"I don't really understand," Jill said sleepily.

"That's okay," Phoebe said, tucking the pink blanket gently around the small girl. "For a long time I didn't either. But one day you will. Just like me."

Phoebe stood up and grinned at Julie.

"And once you get it," she whispered to Jill, "it makes for a pretty amazing equation."

CHAPTER 31

WEDNESDAY, DAY 24

The final bell rang, and Evan joined the crowd of students heading to their lockers. The halls of Granville smelled inexplicably like boiled sneakers, though that was not bothering Evan as much as the death glares that had been coming his way all week. He kept his head down as he grabbed his coat and backpack from his locker, then started down the hall again.

"Hi, Evan," Avery said as she passed with a few other fifth graders.

At least someone was talking to him.

"Hi," he called, then had to sidestep a group of third graders.

"That's the boy who ruined the chocolate sale," one of the girls said, pointing at Evan.

Great, even the little kids hated him.

"He's the worst," a boy in the group said, shaking his finger at Evan, who hustled around the corner.

Evan really hoped the reparations the DeerVilles were doing would fix things because he was tired of being the big jerk of Granville. Though at least he wasn't alone, because here came Phoebe, a silver headband in her short black curls and her backpack slung over one shoulder.

"This better work," she told Evan as they walked together past room 112, the once and hopefully future sales headquarters. "Because I am tired of being enemy number one."

"Yeah, I feel like Magneto," Evan agreed as they walked out the front doors of the school and into the cold.

"Who?" Phoebe asked blankly.

"Don't worry about it," Evan said. He'd tell Gabe later—Gabe knew X-Men, so he'd get it. And maybe they could also get back to that conversation about who was more like Wolverine because it obviously wasn't Gabe.

"Great job with your secret sale by the way," Phoebe said. The two headed down the snowy sidewalk toward Deerfield.

"Thanks," Evan said, smiling at her from behind his hat and scarf. Selling with Gabe had been fun, though he was really looking forward to non-secret sales that the four of them would do together, just as soon as permission had been granted.

"Isn't it weird to think that we've only been doing the Challenge for twenty-four days?" Phoebe mused. "It feels like so much longer."

"Tell me about it," Evan said. It seriously felt like a lifetime ago that he had eagerly signed up to run for co-captain in hopes of making friends at his new school by wowing everyone with his sales skills.

It was an understatement to say things hadn't gone how he'd imagined.

Finally arriving at Deerfield, they walked up the steps and into the lobby where Julie and Gabe were waiting.

"I think I tracked down enough Fantastic Five bars for everyone who works in the administration office," Julie said, the box of bars cradled under one arm. "And I think—"

"Hi, Julie," Phoebe said, giggling.

"She's been like this all afternoon," Gabe said, rolling his eyes but grinning.

"Okay, sorry, but I just want to make sure—" Julie began, pressing a hand to her chest.

"We'll do it right, we know," Evan said. Then he grinned. "And we will, don't worry. We have the chocolate and we're ready to file or organize supplies or whatever else so the administrators can get a long coffee break."

"I hope they don't ask us to empty the garbage cans in the office," Gabe said, grimacing at Evan. He laughed, and Evan felt the cozy warmth of sharing an inside joke.

"Tell me about it," he said.

"I was thinking we should do our first sale today at Kid Kicks Karate school because we'll get there around five, if everything works out, and there should be a bunch of kids who want chocolate," Julie said as they started toward the main office.

"Sounds good," Evan agreed. He pulled off his hat and coat as they walked. "And maybe we'd also have time to go to the pharmacy because it's right next door."

"Do you guys want to come over for dinner on Friday?" Phoebe asked as they walked down the hall together. "My dad makes amazing lasagna and we can game-plan for a big sales weekend."

Phoebe said it casually, but the words stopped Evan in his tracks. Yes, the Challenge had gone differently than he'd imagined. But the thing he wanted most had happened: He had made friends, good friends. Friends who invited him over for dinner. Friends he trusted so much he had told them the Banana Butt story. Friends who stuck by him even when he messed up, a lot.

"You coming?" Gabe asked. The three of them had arrived at the door to the main office and were looking back at Evan.

"Yeah," Evan said, as something else occurred to him. Gabe, Julie, and Phoebe liked him not for his pranks or his sales skills but because he was Evan Black. With the three of them, just being Evan was enough. And while Evan wanted to rack up awesome sales numbers for the next six days, and figured that he'd pull a few more pranks before the year was over, it felt pretty good that even if neither of those things happened, Julie, Phoebe, and Gabe would still like him.

"I'm coming," he said, grinning as he came up to his friends, and the four of them walked into the office.

And then they stopped. Because standing in front of the counter were Ms. Chase and Mr. Ryan.

"We had a feeling you might show up here," Ms. Chase said, tipping her head slightly as she looked at each of them.

Evan's breath was stuck in his chest as he waited to hear why the faculty advisors to the Challenge had tracked them down. Were they angry the DeerVilles were making reparations? Had they heard about the secret sale?

"We heard you've been going to the people who were hurt by your pranks, to make amends," Mr. Ryan said, pressing his hands together.

"We wanted to make reparations," Julie said. Her face was pinker than it had been after the cold and she was tugging furiously on the end of her braid.

"I like the impressive vocab word," Ms. Chase said, and Evan remembered that she was a fifth-grade English teacher. "And we both like the impressive actions."

At that Evan could breathe just a little.

"Especially cleaning out the Dumpster," Mr. Ryan added, grinning. "That took guts."

"And a strong stomach," Gabe added.

Evan couldn't help snickering at that.

"Mr. Samuels and Mr. Claiborne weren't sure you kids would get the job done, but you did and you did it well," Ms. Chase said, shaking her head and smiling a half smile.

"And Ms. Fahadi had some very nice things to say about your story-hour visit," Mr. Ryan said.

"She said she believed in second chances," Phoebe said hopefully, shifting her weight from one foot to the other.

Ms. Chase grinned. "I take it by making that statement you are asking if we also believe in second chances, after reparations have been made."

Phoebe bit her lip and nodded, and now Evan's breath

was stuck again as he waited for the answer that would determine their fate.

"Yes," Mr. Ryan said. "We believe that you guys have earned a second chance. The Challenge is back on!"

Evan whooped as he and Phoebe high-fived. Julie was beaming while Gabe pumped his fist in the air. They'd done it—they'd saved the Challenge!

"We won't let you down," Julie promised Ms. Chase and Mr. Ryan, opening the chocolate box to hand out Fantastic Five to the administrators.

"And we're going to break the previous sales record," Phoebe added. "It's nine hundred twelve bars, and we're going to leave that number in the dust."

"But not by pulling pranks," Evan added hastily, wanting to be sure that was very clear. "By making sales."

"We'll start as soon as we've made reparations to everyone here," Julie said, looking around the office.

"Go beat that record," Mr. Finley, an administrative assistant, said with a smile. He was sitting right behind the counter and had cheered when Mr. Ryan made the announcement that the Challenge would happen. "That's all the reparations we need."

"Not so fast! We'll take the chocolate too," Ms. Cho, at the desk behind Mr. Finley, added, and they all laughed.

Once the Fantastic Five bars had been distributed to everyone in the office, Ms. Chase and Mr. Ryan led team DeerVille upstairs to the closet in Mr. Ryan's room, where their sales sheets and boxes of chocolate waited. Evan's mouth watered as he took in the towering stack of Fantastic Fives—he'd be buying a box today for sure. He and the other DeerVilles had a lot to celebrate after all.

"We'll make sure that the reinstatement of the Challenge is announced first thing tomorrow," Mr. Ryan said as they gathered supplies.

"Great," Phoebe said, pulling on her coat. "It'll be nice to walk down the hall without everyone glaring at us."

"Seriously," Evan agreed. He was definitely looking forward to that.

"Is everybody ready?" Julie asked. She was standing by the door, coat on and Fantastic Five box in hand. Evan, Phoebe, and Gabe joined her.

"Okay, Team DeerVille, go make our town proud!" Ms. Chase called.

And the four friends and co-captains headed out into the snowy afternoon to do just that.

CHAPTER 32

SALE COMPLETE
Team DeerVille: 1,007

"Welcome, everyone," Mayor Pellegrino called out from the stage in the auditorium of the community center. The entire town of Scottsdale filled up the room and spilled out into the hall and down the steps of the big brick building. On the stage sat representatives from not one but two schools: Deerfield and Granville. And in the first row, sitting next to each other, were team co-captains Julie, Phoebe, Gabe, and Evan.

"It is my pleasure to see all of you here to celebrate the incredible work and dedication of our students," the mayor said, turning to smile at them. "This year I'm thrilled to announce that they have sold a record-setting number of chocolate bars, raising over twenty thousand dollars for two local charities!"

The cheering was so loud the mayor had to step back from the mic and wait for it to die down.

"Yes, I'm as impressed as you are," the mayor said when she could be heard once more. "And now, before I present the checks to each of these charities, the four team leaders of this impressive sale have asked if they could address you themselves." She beckoned Gabe, Phoebe, Julie, and Evan to come up beside her.

"First we wanted to say thanks to everyone for supporting the sale," Evan said, kicking off the short speech the four of them had prepared.

"It's thanks to all of you that we've been able to raise so much," Gabe added. At first he spoke too quietly to be heard, so Julie poked him and he repeated himself.

Then Julie stepped up to the mic. "But we also need to apologize," she said. "Before we joined forces, our competition got out of hand. Very out of hand. And we're really sorry about that."

"We hope that even though we messed it up for a while there," Phoebe said, "that Scottsdale will continue to have the Chocolate Challenge and that next year's team will earn even more than we did. And put me down for a box of the Lava bar because I've already eaten the ones I got this year."

"Let's give it up for your team leaders!" Mayor Pellegrino said, and the entire town stood on its feet to give them a magnificent ovation.

After the checks had been presented and each charity spoke of the ways they would use the funds to help their organizations, the mayor thanked everyone. And with that, the Chocolate Challenge was officially over.

"That was pretty cool," Evan said as the four of them stood on the stage.

"Yeah," Gabe agreed.

"What do we do now?" Phoebe asked.

Julie grinned. "Well, the annual Valentine's carnation fund-raiser is coming up in a few months," she said. "Maybe we should start getting ready now."

The other three team members groaned.

"No more sales," Phoebe said.

"Or contests," Evan agreed.

"Or pranks," Gabe said, giving Evan a meaningful look.

"Okay, well, then how about this?" Julie asked, pulling something out of her bag. When they saw what she held in her hand, the other three leaders cheered. Julie handed Phoebe a Lava bar, Gabe a S'mores bar, and Evan a Sweet and Simple, and peeled the wrapper off her own Triple Crown.

And then the former team leaders of the annual Scottsdale Chocolate Challenge enjoyed their last chocolate bars of the sale together.

ABOUT THE AUTHOR

Daphne Benedis-Grab is the author of *Army Brats*, *The Angel Tree*, *Clementine for Christmas*, and *Alive and Well in Prague, New York*. She has worked a variety of jobs, including building houses for Habitat for Humanity in Georgia, organizing an after-school tutoring program in San Francisco, and teaching English in China. She grew up in a small town in upstate New York and now lives in New York City with her husband, two kids, and cat. Learn more at www.daphnebg.com.